CHERRY AMES, VETERANS' NURSE

CHERRY AMES NURSE STORIES

CHERRY AMES VETERANS' NURSE

By

HELEN WELLS

SPRINGER PUBLISHING COMPANY
New York

Copyright © 1946 by Grosset & Dunlap, Inc.
Copyright © renewed 2007 by Harriet Schulman Forman
Springer Publishing Company, LLC

All rights reserved.

No part of this publication may be reproduced, stored in a retrieval system, or transmitted in any form or by any means, electronic, mechanical, photocopying, recording, or otherwise, without the prior permission of Springer Publishing Company, LLC.

Springer Publishing Company, LLC
11 West 42nd Street, 15th Floor
New York, NY 10036-8002

Acquisitions Editor: Sally J. Barhydt
Production Editor: Matthew Byrd
Cover design by Takeout Graphics, Inc.
Composition: Techbooks

    08   09   10/5   4   3   2

Library of Congress Cataloging-in-Publication Data

Wells, Helen, 1910-
  Cherry Ames, veterans' nurse / by Helen Wells.
    p. cm.— (Cherry Ames nurse stories)
  Summary: When the war is over, Cherry comes home to Hilton,
Illinois, and faces the challenge of caring for wounded veterans.
  ISBN 0-8261-0400-2
  [1. Nurses–Fiction.   2. Hospitals–Fiction.   3. Veterans–Fiction.
4. Illinois–Fiction.]   I. Title.

PZ7.W4644Cl 2006
[Fic]—dc22

                                                            2006022324

Printed in the United States of America by Bang Printing

Contents

	Foreword	vii
I	Home-Coming	1
II	Surprises	17
III	Jim	28
IV	April Fool	39
V	A Little Boy	55
VI	Midge's Big Romance	68
VII	First Test	84
VIII	Week End	105
IX	Clues	115
X	A Turn for the Better	133
XI	Wade Comes to Town	140
XII	Strange Story	161
XIII	Midnight Discovery	173
XIV	The Happiest Day	188
XV	End and Beginning	203

Foreword

Helen Wells, the author of the Cherry Ames stories, said, "I've always thought of nursing, and perhaps you have, too, as just about the most exciting, important, and rewarding, profession there is. Can you think of any other skill that is *always* needed by everybody, everywhere?"

I was and still am a fan of Cherry Ames. Her courageous dedication to her patients; her exciting escapades; her thirst for knowledge; her intelligent application of her nursing skills; and the respect she achieved as a registered nurse (RN) all made it clear to me, I was going to follow in her footsteps and become a nurse—nothing else would do. Thousands of other young people were motivated by Cherry Ames to become RNs as well. Cherry Ames motivated young people on into the 1970s, when the series ended. Readers who remember reading these books in the past will enjoy rereading them now—whether or not they chose nursing as a career—and perhaps sharing them with others.

My career has been a rich and satisfying one, during which I have delivered babies, saved lives, and cared for people in hospitals and in their homes. I have worked at the bedside and served as an administrator. I have published journals, written articles, taught students, consulted, and given expert testimony. Never once did I regret my decision to enter nursing.

During the time that I was publishing a nursing journal, I became acquainted with Robert Wells, brother of Helen Wells. In the course of conversation I learned that Ms. Wells had passed on and left the Cherry Ames copyright to Mr. Wells. Because there is a shortage of nurses here in the US today, I thought, "Why not bring Cherry back to motivate a whole new generation of young people? Why not ask Mr. Wells for the copyright to Cherry Ames?" Mr. Wells agreed, and the republished series is dedicated both to Helen Wells, the original author, and to her brother, Robert Wells, who transferred the rights to me. I am proud to ensure the continuation of Cherry Ames into the twenty-first century.

The final dedication is to you, both new and old readers of Cherry Ames: It is my dream that you enjoy Cherry's nursing skills as well as her escapades. I hope that young readers will feel motivated to choose nursing as their life's work. Remember, as Helen Wells herself said: there's no other skill that's *"always* needed by everybody, everywhere."

Harriet Schulman Forman, RN, EdD
Series Editor

CHAPTER I

Home-Coming

ALMOST—ALMOST THERE! A VERY FEW MINUTES MORE, with the train hurtling and whistling past the wintry prairie farms—in minutes she would be there!

Cherry stood up unsteadily in the train aisle and pulled her luggage down from the overhead rack. She straightened her khaki hat on her black curls, straightened her Army Nurse's jacket, drew on her leather gloves. Then she sat on the very edge of her plush chair. The train was slowing down now. Johnson's big barn and the outskirts of Hilton skidded past. Cherry's cheeks were very red, her dark eyes brilliant.

"New York—London—Panama—the Pacific—I've seen them all—I've flown over Europe—" Cherry thought "—but—well, Hilton, Illinois, I'm coming *home*!" For this was the destination and the day she had been dreaming of.

She stood up and paced to the noisy vestibule, too excited to sit still. The little old conductor out there smiled and shouted at her:

"I guess you been away a long time, hey, Lieutenant?"

She shouted back over the iron clanking, "Too long!"

"I bet your maw and paw'll be at the station with a band!"

A wave of homesickness caught her. Cherry visualized her family waiting for her on the platform. "They'll be there!" she shouted to the conductor. "They know I always come in on the Wabash line!"

Now the train was cutting through Hilton's side streets. Cherry looked out achingly at well-remembered picket fences, sooty frame houses, cars waiting at the railroad crossings. She hungrily breathed in the acrid soft-coal smoke, curling along the flat prairie land.

Finally the train heaved a great puff and the wheels creaked to a stop along the station shed. Cherry eagerly looked out at the people scattered along the platform, seeking familiar faces.

"Hi-i-il-*ton!*" the conductor called. "*Hil*ton! Have a good reunion, Lieutenant," and he lifted Cherry's bags off the train, and gave her a hand down.

Cherry stood there in the wind. She looked up and down the platform but no one came toward her. Behind her, the train was already slowly pulling away. She watched, rather wistfully, other travelers being met, kissed, hurried off to cars. Well, my goodness, where was *her* family? Here came a slim woman in furs—at last! Why, her mother must have a new coat. No, it was not her mother, after all. The woman passed her by.

"Now, isn't this a fine thing!" Cherry thought in humorous disgust. "Heroine returns from the wars and not even a little old yellow dog comes to greet her. Of all occasions for us to get our arrangements jumbled!"

She resolutely picked up her bags and walked against the February wind to the taxi stand, where one lone black sedan waited. But the driver was not there. Just as well, Cherry decided; she would wait around a few minutes, in case her family had been delayed.

No one appeared, however, except a lanky youth.

"Taxi, ma'am?"

"Yes." Cherry gave the address of her gray house, and climbed in the back seat. She did feel a little disgruntled. Probably her family was down at the Illinois Central depot, or at the Big Four. But they knew she always came on this route, on the Wabash line. Why, she had clearly wired them: "Arriving Wabash four Thursday afternoon. Love."

Well, she would forget about it. But as the car pulled out onto the snowy street, Cherry sat up sharply. Maybe her family *could not* come! Maybe someone was terribly ill. Or they had moved away and forgotten to write her.

She checked herself and chuckled. "Nice worrying, Ames. Hold on for ten minutes more and then it will all be cleared up. I'll just say hello to Hilton, meantime."

The town, as she rode through the downtown section, seemed smaller and shabbier than she remembered it. Most of the two and three-story stores needed paint, the cars parked at the curb were old and had patched tires. But people walked along at an easier pace, their faces relieved and relaxed—now that the war was over and won.

Now in peacetime there were fewer men in Army uniform around the square. A young soldier proudly pushed a baby carriage. Headlines on the newsstands still gravely underscored the long, hard work of making this peace a permanent peace. But there was a new happiness here at home.

"It's an end and a beginning," Cherry realized. "We'll have to get our wounded veterans cured—start our lives and work all over on a peacetime basis. This war has left us plenty of responsibilities."

Cherry saw a knot of people standing at the corner of East Main and Weatherbee, where a Big Four train had stopped right in the middle of the street. Cherry craned her neck. Yes, a dozen or so people, some carrying big bouquets of flowers, bright against the snow, accompanied by children with little flags, and the inevitable dogs, tails wagging. Didn't she recognize some of those people? But her taxi turned a corner and bounced up her own street so fast she could not be sure.

"Some veteran is being received in style," Cherry thought. She wondered if Hilton laid claim to any generals or heroes. Certainly an Army nurse like herself would not rate a welcoming committee and bouquets—"though it would be nice if someone at least said hello to me!"

At her house, Cherry paid the taximan and scampered up the frozen porch steps. Dropping her luggage, she put her finger on the doorbell and kept it there.

No one answered. There were no friendly faces or shouts from the neighbors' houses, either. Nothing, nothing at all.

With hands that shook a little, Cherry fished in her purse for her key—which she had carried around the world with her, a talisman of home—and opened the front door. As she stepped into the front hall (yes, there was the same mahogany furniture—at least the Ameses still lived here) an unknown woman came toward her crying:

"Go away! You can't come bustin' into strange houses!"

Cherry gasped, took one look at this big husky woman in an apron, and then did something she had not done in all her stern Army years. Cherry's face puckered up and her eyes filled with tears.

"I live here!" she wailed, tears splashing off her red cheeks.

"Flapdoodle! *I* never seed you afore!" The woman folded her arms. "Besides, look at your messy overshoes.

I can't have you trackin' up my clean floors. Can't you see the folks 're going to have a party here?"

Cherry stopped sniffling long enough to look around. Sure enough, the familiar rooms shone, trays of refreshments were laid out, flowers and leaves were everywhere.

"The—the party's for *me!*" Cherry sputtered.

"'Tis not. Mis' Ames says a *soldier's* comin' home."

Despite those salty tears, Cherry had to giggle. "I'm Cherry Ames," she explained. "I'm a soldier—an Army Nurse. And I *live here!*"

"Far's I'm concerned," the be-aproned woman announced, "you could be Mary Ames or you could be Dolores the three-headed wonder. Now git!"

And she held open the door and pointed. "Git!"

Cherry sat herself down on the bottom step of the curving staircase in the hall and clasped her knees. Her giggles exploded into laughter. "I won't git! Who are you anyway?"

"I'm Velva Marcy from a farm down near Turkey Run, and I help out Mis' Ames. And b'lieve you me, when she hears about you—"

Cherry knew plenty of farm people but none like this Velva. She leaned against the banister and laughed so hard that her sides hurt and her hat fell down over her eyes.

"Plumb crazy," muttered the woman.

"Some home-coming! Where is my mother?"

HOME-COMING

"Down to the railroad."

"Which railroad?"

"*The* railroad."

Cherry asked carefully, "Did she carry flowers? Did about a dozen other people go with her?"

"Why, yes, that's so." The buxom Velva studied her cautiously. "'Pears like you might be Carrie Ames at that. Well, you kin sit on a chair if you like."

The woman backed away from Cherry and, still suspicious, disappeared into the back of the house. She poked her head out once to call:

"Kindly don't tell on me—if you *are* Sairy Ames."

Cherry crumpled up again. She laughed until the crystal chandelier vibrated. Then she lay back on the stairs, weak from laughing so much. It was in this undignified position that her parents and the neighbors discovered her.

They surged in the front door, faces exasperated, shifting the enormous bouquets from one arm to another. When they saw Cherry, a cry went up: "She's home!"... "—missed her—the other line!"... "Cherry! Oh, poor darling," her mother was saying, half crying, half laughing.

Cherry had sprung up and reached Mrs. Ames first. She kissed her pretty, dark-haired mother, then was swept into her father's bear hug. Young Midge Fortune, her motherless friend, whirled her into a loving embrace. The neighbors drew her into their excited midst.

More people were arriving, too, and Cherry's hand was shaken by so many people, so fast, that she was confused.

"Please—please excuse me," Cherry stammered. "If I could just—" She fled into the dining room, away from the crowd.

Her parents followed, with Midge, and smilingly shut the door.

"They are all so eager to see you, dear," her mother explained. "So proud."

Cherry looked into her mother's tender dark eyes, smiled into her father's level blue ones. Then she took her mother's hand and drew a deep breath.

"I'm home. Just think—home." She asked anxiously, "Are you all all right?"

"We've been fine. Are *you* all right?"

"Oh, yes. Just a little dazed, I guess." She added, murmuring, "I can't believe I'm really home."

Under the commonplace words was a great deal of love. Their smiles were tremulous. Cherry kept looking around, almost wonderingly, at the big family table, the bay window banked with green plants, all the familiar things—no longer quite familiar. "You have new curtains," she said slowly. "And the clock is gone." This was home but changed while she was away—grown a little strange.

She looked at her parents, rather fearfully seeking signs of change in them too. Had they grown away from her? But her mother was still youthful looking, and her brown eyes were as warm and understanding as ever. Only a few weary shadows in her face betrayed the nights her mother had not slept when Cherry and her twin brother Charlie were in combat zones. The years of war strain showed more markedly on Cherry's businesslike father. His fair hair was mostly gray now. Still, the same old humor lighted his face. Cherry blew out a small laugh of relief.

"H'lo, Cherry," Midge piped up. She waved a freckled hand.

Cherry had to grin. She pulled young Midge over to her and yanked the girl's light-brown hair. "How are you, tomboy?"

Midge muttered "Fine," then burst out, "I'm so glad you're home!"

"Of course I'm not pleased, not a bit," said Mr. Ames. His smile broadened. "Hey! She's here! What do you know? She's *home!*"

"Hurray!" Midge spun around, her full short skirt standing straight out. "Cherry's here! Cherry's back!"

Mrs. Ames stood there, smiling and shaking her head, as if she too still could not believe this happiness. "We're so lucky, Cherry. So grateful. Plenty of young men and women will never come back."

"Or"—Cherry frowned—"some are coming back hurt and maimed and sick. That's what my work is going to be, now. Helping those veterans get well." She ruefully shook her head and her dark curls danced. "We've been lucky about Charlie. Where is that flier brother of mine?"

Her father replied, "Still out in the Pacific. He's flying supplies to the Army of Occupation in Japan. Even though the war is over, Charlie still may be gone a long time."

"It's all right," Mrs. Ames said fervently. "I don't care how long Charles has to stay in the Army—he's survived! Next to that, nothing else is important. Oh, we've been lucky!"

Cherry started to speak but decided against saying anything so somber. She was thinking of the wounded men whom she, as an Army Nurse, had helped—literally hundreds of young men who really might never have come back except for her nursing.

Midge tugged at her sleeve. "You look as if you're far, far away," she objected. "Please come back."

Cherry turned and an odd smile formed on her vivid face. "Sorry, Midge. I guess it will take me a little time to change from soldier into civilian. But," she grinned broadly at all of them, "I have no objections to being home—or to having breakfast in bed—or having parties given for me! No objections at all!"

"Well, come on!" Midge bolted for the door.

"Just a minute," Mrs. Ames said. Her warning tone froze Midge's hand on the knob. "I have explanations to make to every neighbor on our block. They—and

HOME-COMING 11

I—should like to know how we all happened to miss Cherry at the train. I *wrote* her to take the Big Four! And I gave Midge that letter to mail!"

Mrs. Ames looked meaningfully at Midge. The teenager stared back with round, scared eyes. The clatter of the reception in the next room sounded very loud.

"Oh, please don't tell on me—not to all those people!"

"Don't tell on me!" came an echo. Velva's woeful face popped out at the pantry door, then vanished.

"What in thunder—" Mr. Ames started.

"So this mix-up was your doing, Midge? And Velva too? Velva?" Mrs. Ames was mystified. "But, Midge, how did you manage to ruin Cherry's celebration?"

"I didn't mean to," Midge blurted out. "I simply forgot to mail your special-delivery letter. I just remembered it *this minute.*"

"But, Velva—?"

"I told her to git!" Velva admitted in chagrin as she emerged from the pantry.

"Well, I got home in spite of all of you!" Cherry teased. "Now I suppose you'll try to put me out!"

Midge apologized profusely. Velva was nearly in tears.

"Never mind, never mind," Mrs. Ames hastily soothed everybody. "Will, please get these youngsters in there to the reception. It sounds as if the whole town is here—and we're not even in there to receive them—Velva isn't serving the tea—Such hosts!"

Cherry's father flung open the double doors and Cherry faced a sea of old friends and acquaintances. A wave of voices, smiles, handclasps, engulfed her. Here were her old school friends—here were the neighbors for blocks around—her three favorite teachers from high school days! Even the children and the very old people had come. Warm voices, warm eyes, welcomed Cherry home. Now all the bouquets were heaped into her arms until her flushed face was almost lost behind the flowers.

"I don't deserve all this fuss," Cherry insisted. She felt no triumph, only rejoicing at being home again. "Oh, it's so good to see all of you! Yes, Mother, please take the flowers—This is really a home-coming!"

And still the doorbell rang, and more people pressed into the Ameses' big, hospitable house. Cherry accepted welcomes, compliments, toasts. "Our globe-trotter ..." ... "Why Cherry, I knew you when you were knee-high to a grasshopper"... "Our son-in-law wrote that you treated him—under fire!"

Then a deep, slow voice at her elbow said, "Well done, my dear."

Cherry whirled. "Dr. Joe!"

There he stood: small, elderly, tired, his gentle face still glowing with an inner fire—the gray-haired doctor who had shaped Cherry's beliefs and Cherry's life.

"Dr. Joe," Cherry said happily. Against merry protests, she disengaged herself from a group of friends and led Dr. Joseph Fortune to a quiet corner beside the fireplace.

"Ah, Cherry, child, it surely is good to see you," he said shakily.

Cherry smiled back gratefully, almost humbly, at her old friend and mentor. Dr. Fortune, Midge's widowed father, was Cherry's lifelong neighbor. Of all the people in this teeming room, he alone fully understood where Cherry had been, what she had done—and why. For Dr. Joe, through his own devotion to medicine, had inspired Cherry to serve others through nursing.

Cherry held out her khaki sleeve next to Dr. Fortune's gray flannel one.

"You're no longer in uniform, Dr. Joe?"

"I might as well tell you at once."

Dr. Fortune, at the beginning of the war, had given up his research post at Spencer Hospital to discover new medicines for the Army. After working several years in guarded Army laboratories, the elderly doctor recently broke down. Perhaps it was his earlier years of struggle and poverty, when only Cherry recognized the value of his work, that were affecting his health now. At any rate, Dr. Joe was ordered home by Army surgeons to rest for six months. He and Midge were back together in their little cottage.

"I'm not satisfied, Cherry. I feel all at loose ends. Of course I'm doing a little experiment at home—"

"—when you should be resting. Why doesn't Midge make you rest and take care of yourself? I'm going to speak to her."

Cherry could imagine what a slapdash household, what sketchy meals, Midge provided. Yet, it was a heavy assignment for a young girl, who had to go to school too. On the other hand, someone had to help Dr. Joe build up physically. He did look dangerously tired. Cherry made a prompt decision. She had kept an eye on the two lone Fortunes before she went away from Hilton, she could do it again now. Cheerfully she announced to Dr. Joe:

"Guess what? I'm assigned to the Army rehabilitation hospital over at Trumble. That's only thirty miles away. So I can be in Hilton quite a lot—week ends, overnight, holidays. Just you watch this nurse—"

"You're going to be that near!" exclaimed Mrs. Ames. She had come up to offer them cups of punch. "Why, Cherry, that's wonderful."

She summoned Cherry's father and several guests, and repeated this good news. There were cordial responses, followed by all sorts of invitations for Cherry to come to lunch, to dinner, to join the dancing class, head the Girl Scout troop, and even be president of the hobby club.

Cherry said under her breath to Dr. Joe, "This is all so wonderful—all this excitement, but it's awfully wearing."

HOME-COMING

Dr. Joe's eyes twinkled. "Pretty tiresome, being a hero, isn't it?"

A crash sounded from the hallway. Someone was falling down the long flight of stairs, apparently while carrying a full set of dishes. Cherry put down her cup and ran through the assembled guests.

Midge lay at the bottom of the stairs, drenched with punch and yelping. On top of her sprawled Velva, looking surprised and still chewing a mouthful of cake. Bits of dishes, sandwiches, and battered flowers hung miserably on steps, floor, even on the walls.

Cherry and Dr. Fortune picked up Velva first, then rescued Midge. They poked and punched them, while the guests looked on.

"No broken bones," Dr. Fortune said.

"I'm bleeding!" Midge howled.

"All right, Cherry will bind up that scratch," Mrs. Ames said shortly. "What in heaven's name were you two doing?"

Velva said gingerly, "It's a real mess, ain't it?"

"*What*—" Mrs. Ames's eyes were severe and Cherry saw her father retreat into the living room. "What were you up to?"

"We were just taking some of these things up to Cherry's room—I thought I'd have a private little snack with her later—and the vase of water tipped—and we tried to juggle the tray—"

Mrs. Ames pressed her hands to her cheeks. "You're all more nuisance than you're worth! If I had known having Cherry come home meant living through an afternoon like this one—!"

Dr. Joe wryly patted Cherry on the shoulder. "You'd better go back to the peace and quiet of the Army."

She grinned. Then she ripped off her khaki jacket, rolled up her sleeves, and set to wiping Midge's scratched knee.

"I'll pick up the dishes next, Mother," Cherry promised, her black eyes laughing. "Well, this is more natural than all the compliments. Now I know I'm really home!"

CHAPTER II

Surprises

CHERRY TOOK A FIRMER GRIP ON HER SUITCASE, SIGHED, and braced herself for gloom. Then she solemnly pushed open the door into the hospital for wounded veterans.

A burst of jazz out of a loud-speaker startled her. Three boys in khaki jitterbugged past on crutches. One of them casually waved a crutch at her. Cherry stood there in the sunny corridor and blinked.

"One side, please," yelled a masculine voice. A strapping lad in khaki speeded by her in a wheel chair, all but running Cherry down. He rode the chair so fast that the blanket over his lap flapped at the edges as he whizzed by.

"Hey," said Cherry faintly, in her astonishment.

"Hey yourself," said a patient in an Army bathrobe, banging out of a door. His arm was in a huge, awkward cast. In his good hand, he carried a scarlet Cossack costume. A ferocious paper mustache was pasted on his upper lip, and he mouthed his words with care. "Can you tell me where rehearsal is today?"

"Sorry, I can't," Cherry answered and stared after him. He was more or less tap dancing his way along the corridor, to the fast gay beat of the jive.

"I don't believe it!" Cherry said out loud.

She wandered down the corridor, hanging on to her suitcase. The corridor led to an enormous sun-filled sitting room, peaceful with pale-green walls and pictures, a framed jigsaw puzzle on the wall. A few convalescing soldiers sprawled deep in Roman-striped couches and lounge chairs, reading, smoking, playing cards.

"Porter, lady? Carry your bag?" kidded a stalwart young corporal seated on a couch. His leg was missing. He was drinking a glass of milk. Cherry grinned back at him, and swallowed hard. "Porter, lady?"

"Why, yes, porter," she kidded back. "Could you kindly direct me to Track 3 or the Principal Chief Nurse's office?"

"There'll be a slight charge of twenny-fi' cents," the young corporal warned.

A serious young man at a desk looked up from the letter he was writing. "Everything around here'll cost you a slight charge of twenny-fi' cents, Lieutenant."

Cherry put her tongue in her cheek. "All right, I'll open a charge account. Twenny-fi' cent items only. Okay?"

The two patients beamed at her. "Okay. For a nice girl like you, there's no charge. How'd you get in the wrong building, anyway?"

"The military police at the hospital gate wouldn't let my taxi in the grounds. So I got out and walked and—and one brick building looks like another brick building around here. Stop laughing and tell me *where* is the Principal Chief Nurse's office?"

"As a special favor—three buildings down. The little star-shaped building."

"Yes, *sir*. So long."

"See you around, Lieutenant."

Cherry backed out and hurried down the music-filled corridor again. She kept tossing back her black curls and muttering, "Gloom, indeed! It's practically a circus! A three-ringed circus!"

The Principal Chief Nurse's office, however, was hushed and stern and efficient. Cherry waited a few minutes in these offices, watching hard-working administrative nurses at their desks. Then, ushered into an inner private office, Cherry faced a pair of X-ray eyes, belonging to the Principal Chief Nurse herself.

This tiny white-haired Army Nurse was a lieutenant colonel. Cherry saluted and wished she might sit down, for under Colonel Winifred Brown's grim glare, she began to tremble. But Colonel Brown was darting between files and desk; she did not invite Cherry to sit down.

"Two minutes, Lieutenant Ames—then out! I've seen your Army records—you needn't tell me. Now then! We here at Graham Hospital are an Army general hospital. The Army has a responsibility to cure its wounded men and make them fit to earn their own living again. Are you following me, Lieutenant?"

"Y-yes, Colonel Brown."

"Our job is to rebuild broken men, physically and mentally."

Talking at top speed, and at the same time sorting hospital papers, she explained the hospital's work to the new nurse. Colonel Brown did not say, in so many words, that each of these young men was wounded in the defense of his country—nor that to live and work again minus hands, arms, legs, eyes, or hearing was a terrific hurdle—nor that nurses here had to mend spirits as well as bodies, had to find useful and self-sufficient futures for these brave men. But that was what she was really saying, with an extra gruffness in her voice.

Cherry ventured to speak. "I noticed, Colonel," she said, rather puzzled, "the high spirits of the convalescing men."

SURPRISES 21

"They didn't come to us that way!" the Principal Chief Nurse retorted. "What you saw is the result of hard work here. See that *you* treat these men properly!"

Cherry wondered anxiously what was the proper way. She certainly did not want to make mistakes injurious to these men! But Colonel Brown raced on.

"Now. Each Army general hospital specializes. Graham specializes in orthopedics [bone injuries] and some general cases. You will be a floater for two months or more, Lieutenant Ames, until I decide what you're worth as a nurse. Then I will rate you and reassign you—*if* you merit it. You will work eight hours a day, six days a week. We maintain strict military discipline here. Report to Lieutenant Steen at Nurses' Quarters. Any questions? Then that's all. The door out is there." She pointed and picked up her phone. "The general.— Well, get him! And hurry up."

Cherry saluted, marched out double-quick time, and paused to breathe again. She was still trembling.

An administrative nurse half smiled at Cherry and softly confided:

"The general himself quakes at the sight of her!"

Cherry smiled back gratefully. "Where do I go now?"

"Nurses' Quarters is diagonally across the grounds from here. Room 24 is yours. Leave your bag, then see Lieutenant Steen. Good luck!"

Cherry emerged from the star-shaped building feeling very new here, very ignorant and inadequate. She found her way across the far-flung grounds. There were so many of these tall, square brick buildings—so many Red Cross station wagons on the winding hospital roads—so many patients walking along in maroon bathrobes, trench caps, and clumsy GI shoes—above all, so much she had to learn. And learn quickly! Perhaps this Lieutenant Steen would provide some urgently needed advice.

The entrance hall to Nurses' Quarters was deserted. Cherry looked around this enormous bare new building, figured out how the rooms were numbered, climbed a flight of stairs, and located Room 24.

"Hello," Cherry murmured. "Welcome to Room 24."

Her new room was not a particularly welcoming sort of place. It was bare and utilitarian and metallic, with whitewashed walls and shiny new plumbing and a cot. But down at the end of the hall was a nurses' sitting room, and a small kitchen. Anyway, Cherry planned to spend her free days at home in Hilton.

"Lieutenant Ames?" a laconic voice inquired. "Hi, I'm Sally Steen."

Draped in the steel doorway was a lanky girl with hair, eyes, and skin all the same pale tan monotone. Even her voice was flat. She was loose-jointed as a puppet, in her beige-and-white striped seersucker dress. There was something irresistibly droll about her.

"Yes, I'm Cherry Ames. Come in, won't you?"

Lieutenant Steen strolled in. "I'm supposed to show you all around the hospital. I'm the welcoming committee. Welcome. Welcome to Graham Hospital and have a couple of clean towels." She produced towels and bed linen and blankets from a closet shelf. Her face still had no expression, but her pale eyes met Cherry's with a gleam of fun. "The kids here call me Sal."

"Well, Colonel Brown all but called me Hopeless."

"You know, she really is the battle-ax she looks, but don't let her upset you." Sal's angular face screwed up into an engaging smile.

"But I am upset. Or at least puzzled." Cherry forthrightly asked the other nurse about how to treat the wounded men at Graham. "It seems to be an awfully touchy question."

"There's nothing to it," Lieutenant Steen said flatly. "These wounded men are perfectly normal people—only they got hurt, that's all. So treat them normally, the way you'd treat anyone." Sal grunted. "How would *you* like it if people started treating you like a nut, just because you'd had a nervous breakdown or got smashed up in an automobile accident?"

"That's right. I rested a month in Hilton and some people did say some pretty foolish things to me. Yes," said Cherry uncertainly, "I guess I see. But—but—"

"You *will* see," Sal promised. "And right away. We've got a trainload of new patients coming in this afternoon. Come on. Show you the place first."

Sal got her coat from her room a few doors down. Then she ambled down the stairs, whistling, Cherry with her. Cherry could understand how this nonchalant, levelheaded, droll Sal would be tonic for the patients. They went out into the big yard with its bare trees, and entered the closed wooden corridors which connected all of the hospital buildings. This big outside maze ran all over the grounds. Sal explained about this catwalk: left to chapel, dental clinic, Red Cross, cobbler shop; right to Building 5; straight ahead to Buildings 6 and 8. "After that, follow the signs and your nose."

Cherry asked, as they walked, "Any of my old friends here? Ann Evans and Gwen Jones are still in England but"—she eagerly reeled off names of girls she had gone to nursing school with—"Bertha Larsen, Mai Lee, Josie Franklin, Marie Swift, Vivian Warren? Are any of them here?"

Sal carefully and thoughtfully repeated the names without a single error. Either, Cherry thought, Lieutenant Steen had a memory like a steel trap or else her friends were really here. Oh, good!

Sal winked. "—and Vivian Warren. Why, sure! Lots of nice kids here. Lots of good times for everybody. It helps the fellows get well—and we nurses don't mind picnics and games at all."

They turned down another outside corridor, smelling of wood and rain, their footsteps clattering on the boards.

SURPRISES 25

"How's the romance department?" Cherry asked.

"Oh, that," Sal said matter-of-factly. "The men fall in love with us nurses so persistently that we have to transfer from ward to ward every few days. That cures them of a lot of silly ideas."

Cherry burst out laughing. "You're not very romantic!"

"Romantic with a funny face like mine?"

"It's a cute face." Cherry added, "Of course, there'll be a slight charge of twenny-fi' cents for the compli-men't."

Sal propelled her around another corner. "You catch on quick," she approved.

By the time their tour was completed, Cherry had learned that Graham had 6,000 beds (about half of them filled), 100 buildings, 400 acres—that the yard was overrun with squirrels which demanded peanuts—that Officers' Mess hall had flowers and white linen tablecloths and a great many pleasant people in it.

Sal insisted on introducing Cherry around before filling their food trays. She led the newcomer to the first table, where two nurses and a doctor were lunching together. The young Army doctor politely got to his feet.

"This is Lieutenant Cherry Ames," Sal droned. "Cherry, this is Dr. Vivian Warren. I understand you two are old friends."

Cherry was astounded. *Her* Vivian Warren belonged to the feminine gender. Apparently the doctor was astonished too. Certainly he had every right to be. Cherry was no old friend of his: she had never seen him before.

"Isn't Vivian a strange name for a man?" Sal said. "But it's English, y'know. Veddy, veddy British."

Cherry and the young man blinked at each other.

"How do you do, Captain Warren," Cherry said in some confusion. "What an odd coincidence of names."

"How are you, Lieutenant Fruit," said the doctor, equally confused. He looked beseechingly at Sal.

"Not Fruit. Cherry. Ames. Now," continued Sal, smiling a sugary smile at the two Army nurses, "forgive me for introducing you ladies second. This first one is Mai Lee. Say hello, Mai."

The blonde girl took off her glasses, blinked her eyelashes, and said in a Southern accent, "Welcome to Graham, honey chile. We-all ah sho' glad you-all is heah."

Cherry stared despite herself. This was the most unconvincing Southern accent she had ever heard.

"And this pretty gal," Sal intoned, nodding toward the second nurse, "is Josie Franklin."

Cherry's Josie was a perpetually scared little creature. This lovely girl was serene, almost motherly, with long brown hair coiled about her head.

The girl smiled. "Is your name really Cherry?" she asked with interest.

"Would you doubt my word?" Sal started. "Why, I—"

Suddenly Cherry caught on. She certainly did doubt Sal's word! Sal was tagging these three people with the names of Cherry's school friends—and they were playing parts, joining Sal in the joke on Cherry. Naturally they thought Cherry's name too was *not* what Sal said.

Cherry leaned past Sal and looked intensely into their three faces. She stared at them until their eyes grew almost frightened. In ominous tones Cherry whispered:

"No. My name isn't Cherry Ames. I'm really Mad Katie the Ax Killer."

And with that, she marched off to the food counter, leaving three laughing people at the table—and Sal disgustedly bringing up the rear.

CHAPTER III

Jim

AN HOUR LATER, IN AN ADMITTING BUILDING, CHERRY'S mood was sharply changed. The wards in Building 7 were empty, scrubbed, and waiting for patients. It was as quiet and tense in there as the electrically charged stillness before a storm breaks.

Thirty Army nurses stood about on the ground floor: some of them had been rushed off other wards to help. One hundred and five seriously wounded men were expected. Everything was in readiness: small receiving rooms each with six cots freshly made, medications and trays set out on small tables; in the big sitting room there was a supply of milk and coffee and a steam table of hot food. A pile of crutches and wheel chairs stood at the main door. Upstairs, empty wards were ready. Over in Surgery Building, the surgeons were ready for emergencies.

JIM

Cherry waited tensely with the others. Sal Steen stood beside her, and Edith Randall, the pretty brown-haired girl. The doctors were coming in now, in the familiar khaki uniforms. Medical Wacs and medical sergeants brought blank records with each awaited man's name, and stacks of fresh gray pajamas and maroon robes. Very young girls, ward aides, in full-skirted white dresses, filled water pitchers and set food trays. It was uncannily quiet, with rubber heels soundless on linoleum floors, hushed voices, the low tinkle of ward phones.

Edith Randall sighed. "Every time we get these wounded soldiers fresh from overseas," she confessed, "I wish I had become something else than a nurse. Anything else!"

"An animal trainer," Sal suggested.

"A cook. A tightrope dancer," Cherry quipped, to ignore her own nervousness.

They heard the fleet of ambulances bringing the men from the hospital train. The main door was flung wide open. Corpsmen sprang to lift litters off the ambulances, and help down the walking wounded. Nurses and doctors surged forward.

In the crowd of arrivals were men on stretchers, raising their heads from their pillows, some with Purple Hearts pinned on their pajama coats. There were some ambulatory patients: a tall parachutist on crutches with a leg gone and a quick, where-am-I? glance; a man with an arm held rigid and high in a plaster cast who insisted on walking by himself. Here were youths who had stepped on a land mine at Anzio, felt the German 88 in Normandy, or caught a Japanese bullet in the Pacific. Cherry's heart contracted.

"Even though they're finished with war on the battlefields," she realized, "the war is still a very personal thing to them—their fight to recover."

Sal Steen came over to Cherry with lists in her hand. "You are assigned to take care of Travers, Leader, Pernatelli, Blumenthal, and Matthews." She handed Cherry her list of five names. "Room 10."

In a small receiving ward off the big sitting room, Cherry met five pairs of somber eyes. Three of her soldiers lay on cots, one sat in a wheel chair, and one short lad with his arm in a cast stood.

"Hello," Cherry gulped. She forced herself to sound calm. "I'm glad to see you at Graham. We're going to really fix you up here. Let's—let's see how you all stood the train trip. Then you can have Cokes and phone calls and a bath, and then dinner—"

"I could use a Coke," said the lad with the arm cast. He had lively black eyes and his agreeable smile made Cherry feel easier. "Haven't had a Coke in two years."

"What about me?" grumbled a red-haired boy on a cot.

"Here's nickels," Cherry said eagerly, digging into her pocket. "There's a Coke machine in the sitting room. You could get a basket and bring back five, Mr.—Mr.—"

"Ralph Pernatelli. What's your name?—Okay, five Cokes coming up." He sped out the door.

The baldish man in the wheel chair asked, "Do you need any acrobats around here?"

"Huh?" said Cherry. She looked at the enormous plaster cast holding his leg at a rakish angle. Scribbled on it were signatures, dates, a surgeon's drawing of his fractured kneecap, and the name of this soldier's company. "Did you say acrobat?"

"That's me, ma'am." The man's funny, monkeylike face creased into a smile. "Hy Leader from near St. Joe. From a little place where the road gets wider, and that's the one place in all the world where I want to be. Used to belong to a traveling circus. Watch."

Three heads raised off the litters. The thin wiry man in the wheel chair released the brake, spun the wheels, and the chair whirled around on one wheel until his sparse hair blew. He skidded to a stop not an inch from Cherry's toes.

She laughed, but saw two of the men on the litters tremble at these noisy monkeyshines. "Too strenuous for these fellows," she said aside to the acrobat. She started over to the first cot to check temperature, pulse, and respiration. "Better take it easy." The acrobat nodded.

The quiet man looked up at Cherry as she leaned above him to hold his wrist and count his breathing. When she took the thermometer out of his mouth, he said very low:

"I've lost my right hand. Can the hospital really do something for me?"

It was the voice of an educated man, the drawn face of a man in despair.

"We can do a great deal for you," Cherry told him honestly. "You will learn to do practically everything you did before."

"But I'm a teacher—the children might not like an artificial hand—" His whisper trailed off. "How will my own little girl feel about it? And I—I've got to support my wife and child."

"The children will understand, I think. Did they like you before?" Cherry asked him.

"Yes. Very much." He smiled, remembering.

"Then aren't you probably worrying for nothing?" He considered, seemed to half accept this. Cherry patted him on the shoulder and straightened up. "Anyhow, it's too soon to decide this now. Get well first. And you haven't told me your name."

"George Blumenthal." He hesitated. "It could be worse. I saw eighteen men in my company killed around me. I'm pretty lucky." He looked up at Cherry from his pillow with the ghost of a smile. "May I—may I phone my wife in Indianapolis? She'll help me pull through this."

"You certainly may. I'll have a phone brought and plugged in here for you."

Cherry stepped to the door, hailed a ward aide, and nearly collided with Ralph Pernatelli and his basket of Cokes. Ralph cheerfully distributed Cokes with his free arm while Cherry turned back to the two men on the cots.

The redheaded fellow was tall, thin, and freckled, only about nineteen, and in a full body cast from his armpits to his feet. He drawled at Cherry:

"I suppose you're a Do-Gooder."

"Heaven forbid. I'm a nurse," Cherry answered and popped the thermometer into his mouth. He glared at her out of brilliantly blue eyes.

"What's the matter with you, tough guy?" she asked as she removed the thermometer.

"Broken back."

Cherry was careful not to offer sympathy. "We'll get you fixed up. What's your name, Red?"

"Bailey Matthews. Ranch hand from Texas. And don't give me any pep talks!"

"I wouldn't dare. I'm scared to death of you," Cherry mocked. "Have a Coke? Want to phone?"

"Naw. Go away and let me alone."

"The same to you, tough guy, only double," and Cherry made a horrible face at him and walked away.

He grinned. "All right. All right. Hey!"

Cherry turned back to him.

"Those phone calls free?"

"Yes."

"What's the catch?"

"No catch."

Ralph Pernatelli said comfortably, "Pay no attention to sourpuss. He's got a suspicious nature. I only met him on the train but I know."

Hy Leader in the wheel chair spoke up, almost fatherly. "Why don't you call up your sister in Chicago, Red? It's tough but you have to tell your folks sooner or later about that back."

Cherry had more phones brought. The men's faces, their voices, as they struggled to tell their families of their arrival and injuries, were very moving. Cherry turned away, to the young man on the last cot. He lay very still, thinking.

"Wouldn't you like to phone too, soldier?"

"Thank you, ma'am, but no. Jim Travers is the name."

Cherry bent over him. He was the most exhausted physically of any of her little group. His right leg was gone. But that alone was not enough to explain his pinched gray look and weak pulse. He would not look at her, as she checked him over.

"Are you sure you wouldn't like to phone?" Cherry gently asked again.

"Who wants me now, with my leg gone?" He turned his face away.

Cherry understood then that Jim Travers's deepest wound was of the spirit. That would be harder to heal than a leg.

"Your people don't know, then," she murmured.

"Only have my mother. In Oregon. She's teaching in a country school. I was going back to take care of her."

Cherry looked at his dressing and started to change it. "How old are you, Jim Travers?"

"Twenty-two."

Cherry was shocked. At this moment, he looked forty.

"Jim. Listen to me. You think everything is over for you. But that's not true. Give the hospital a chance to help you. Don't give up before you at least give us a fair chance."

"You're very kind, ma'am. But it's no use."

Cherry smiled at him. "Which would you prefer—fried chicken or steak? Or both?"

"I'm not hungry."

"I don't believe you. I'm going to hold a sizzling platter under your nose until you work up an appetite."

But it did not work. The other four men were helped by corpsmen through baths, and into fresh pajamas and robes. Cherry in the meantime made her report to the doctor. Then the paymaster came in to give each man five dollars. It made them feel considerably more independent to have some pocket money, for their pay had not caught up with them. Then dinner was wheeled in, and the soldiers ate with good appetites. Cherry cut the meat for Ralph and the teacher, and fed Bailey Matthews each mouthful with an enormous GI soup spoon. Only Jim Travers did not eat, did not respond. Dinner over, an air of contented well-being spread through Cherry's little receiving ward. Still Jim lay brooding, his face turned to the wall.

"I saw a piano in there," Hy Leader announced, "and I'm going to play it. All right, nurse?"

"Of course it's all right," Pernatelli decided genially. "I'll go along and get me a Coke."

Out they trundled, awkward with wheel chair and arm cast but smiling.

"I could drink three or four more Cokes," Red called. "Hey, Ralph, bring 'em back to me!"

"And a newspaper, please?" said George.

Cherry sat with her three bedridden patients. The afternoon light was fading and she turned on a lamp. It was quiet, with only snatches of talk and music drifting in from the sitting room. Matthews and Blumenthal were telling her how they got hit. They were eager to tell her, in detail. And these men, though badly hurt, were neither afraid nor sorry.

Jim Travers opened his eyes listlessly. Cherry went quickly to his cot.

"Are you in pain?"

"No, ma'am."

Cherry looked down at him. It was apparent that he was facing his loss and that he was going through a crucible. Jim was battling within himself—not only how he was going to tell his mother but how he was going to go on living, a one-legged man.

Those laughing boys she had seen this morning—some of them had arrived here in just such black despondency, such terrible anxiety, as Jim. Yet they had struggled through to a healthier frame of mind. It could be done. Cherry thought hard.

"Jim," she said. "Stop thinking of yourself on a street corner with a little tin cup. Other handicapped people—Edison, Steinmetz, Alec Templeton, Seversky—weren't licked. You've got a future. It starts right here and now, when we move you in a few minutes to your permanent ward—Orthopedic Ward. Now come out of that tailspin!"

His heavy eyes sought hers.

"Look at George Blumenthal. Look at Red," she appealed. "They're up against it too. But they haven't lost their grip. You're going to depress them if you don't snap out of this."

"Yes, that's so." He said slowly, "Do you really believe I'll ever be good for anything?"

"If you want to, you will. Determination helps."

Jim closed his eyes again. There was no telling what he was thinking.

Cherry thought of the long, hard road ahead for Jim, and for all these young men, until they could be once more useful and independent. Much of their progress would depend on her.

"This won't be nursing of the starched uniform and white cap kind," Cherry warned herself. "This is going to be a fight for these boys' whole future lives!"

CHAPTER IV

April Fool

BEING A FLOATER WAS FUN. CHERRY REALLY BEGAN TO know the hospital, by being assigned daily to different wards. Now, on this cool wet morning of April first, she was going to see still another new wing. For with the six A.M. rising bell in Nurses' Quarters had come a knock at Cherry's door. Sal Steen lolled there in pajamas, her pale-taffy hair dangling in her eyes.

"Cherry, will you be a good guy and do an errand for me? It'll have to be on your lunch hour since it's not your official business. I wouldn't ask you except that I'm going to be very busy today."

Cherry had pried open her black eyes with her fingers. "Who could refuse you, my sweet?"

"Well, will you go over to the Nephalogy Supply Room and get me six grams of tetrathyazide and bring it to Lieutenant Lewis on Ward 2D2?"

"Nephalogy?" Cherry repeated disbelievingly. "Tetrathyazide? What are those? Never heard of 'em. You're making them up."

"Oh, we have a lot of new stuff around here. New things all the time. Around lunch hour, hmm? And—and—don't miss your lunch on my account, though."

"Don't worry. I consider food an all-star attraction. You couldn't begin to compete."

"Well, thanks," Sal had said weakly and trailed back to her own room.

Cherry suspected Sal of being up to her usual tricks. So, as she did official errands all morning, Cherry inquired about this unofficial business.

It was early when she stopped by the physiotherapy rooms, where she delivered a patient for water spray massage to revive deadened nerves in his leg. She asked one of the husky physiotherapists about Sal's instructions.

"Nephalogy?" This sturdy girl started running the complicated sprays. "Yes, I believe there is such a place. But I wouldn't know as much about it as a regular nurse, or doctor."

So when Cherry went way across the grounds to the huge general operating facilities, to watch a patient being brought back to his ward still under anesthetic, she asked a surgical nurse.

"Nephalogy Supply Room? Sure you don't mean Neurology?" Then the nurse said, "Oh, yes, of course. Nephalogy. But I'm not sure where it's located."

"And tetrathyazide?" Cherry inquired suspiciously. "Is there such a medicine?"

One of the surgeons, overhearing, said, "Certainly. If they haven't it at the Nephalogy Supply Room, ask for it at the general medical supply room or the pharmacy."

"Thank you, sir." She felt rather embarrassed that the surgeon had to correct her ignorance. But now, at least, she was getting some place. It was just a matter of locating the Nephalogy Supply Room.

Back she went across the yard, this time heading for the star-shaped building and some reports. It was good to be walking out of doors this fresh, damp morning. The first, sharp yellow-green shoots embroidered gaunt tree branches. Sparrows hopped, twittering, on the wet brown earth. It was a long hike, and Cherry arrived at the offices out of breath.

She had never been in this particular office before. Here was a corps of typists, and other young women working at the filing cabinets. Apparently all the confidential records of patients, medicines, and inner hospital workings were kept here under lock and key.

Over the clatter of typewriters, Cherry said to the first typist in the row, "Can you tell me where to get Captain Braden's reports?"

The typist was a mousy person, neat and colorless. "I'll get them for you, Lieutenant. Come with me."

She led Cherry into an inner office and took keys from her pocket. She explained:

"I'm the head typist, sort of the office supervisor, really, even though I sit there and type with the rest of the girls."

Cherry was not interested in this woman's self-importance. She accepted the reports. "And you want Captain Braden to return them to—?"

"To me. Margaret Heller."

"Yes, Miss Heller. Oh, by the way. Since you're at the nerve center of the hospital—since you are a sort of guardian of information"—Cherry said ironically and Miss Heller gave a modest laugh—"can you tell me where Nephalogy Supply Room is? For medical supplies?"

"It must be Building 23. That's where all the medical supply rooms are."

Here was definite information at last. Cherry followed the head typist or supervisor or whatever she was out of the inner office and back into the crowded typing room. She was about to leave when a soldier with an empty sleeve blocked the doorway. He was carrying a box for correspondence.

"Oh, did our post office send you over?" Miss Heller said. "Well, thank you, but I'm afraid—you—I see you've lost an arm."

The soldier's face turned bitter. "That so? It was there the last time I looked."

There was a ghastly silence as some of the girls who had heard stopped typing.

Cherry went on to Neurosurgery shaking her curly head. How could that Heller say such a hurtful thing? Small wonder the boy gave her a withering answer.

Back at operating facilities, in the Neurosurgery, or nerve surgery, wing, Cherry briefly saw Captain Braden through a glass dome. He was doing an operation for fingers that would not bend, mending both nerves and bone. Cherry was fascinated but trotted off obediently. She had to clear up a question with one of the hospital dietitians, before she would be free, on lunch hour, to get Sal her medicine.

"And my feet are already protesting," she told a squirrel that stopped her on the path. She dug into her pockets where, in self-defense, she had learned to stow peanuts. The squirrel ate, and scampered away.

On the stroke of noon, with the sun shining out in full glory, Cherry hiked another half mile in a hurry to Building 23. Two other nurses, looking as new here as Cherry felt, burst in the door with her. She heard them inquiring of an attendant for things she had never dreamed existed.

"And I'd like to know where Nephalogy is," Cherry said.

The attendant said they had all better go up to the general supply room.

A flustered Army pharmacist was in charge behind a counter. He turned away the other two nurses because they lacked written orders for their requests. They forlornly left. Cherry refused to be turned away.

"Six grams of tetrathyazide," she said stubbornly.

"Of what? There's no such thing!" the man said.

"Isn't this Nephalogy?"

"Young lady, are you kidding me? Or is somebody kidding you? All morning I've had idiotic requests." He ran his hands through his hair.

Not much help to be had from him, Cherry decided. Perhaps she could reach Sal or Lieutenant Lewis on Ward 2D2 and confirm her facts. She asked the pharmacist's permission to use his phone.

"Lieutenant Steen is off the ward for lunch," said Sal's ward.

Operator said, "There's no such ward as 2D2."

With growing suspicion, Cherry asked for Lieutenant Lewis.

"We have no Lewis listed," said Operator.

Cherry hung up with a bang. It echoed through the big deserted room.

"Mr. Pharmacist, I was asked to come to a place which doesn't exist—to get a medicine which doesn't exist—to bring to a person who doesn't exist—on a ward that isn't there!"

APRIL FOOL

The pharmacist merely persisted in looking glum.

"Today is April Fool," Cherry reminded him gently. "Hmm. This appears to be the stock joke, to be played on all the new people. And gosh, the whole hospital staff is in on the game!" She started to laugh. "How they all cooperated in fooling me! Nurses—even that dignified surgeon—with such straight faces—!" She appealed to the pharmacist, "Don't you think it's funny?"

He said soberly, "I can usually see a joke. But not in here. We have a lot of valuables here under lock and key. I don't want any intruders who might help themselves to these medicines." He waved to the many locked doors. "That's why I don't think it's a good idea for people to be wandering in and out of here."

Cherry agreed politely but she was thinking that April Fools' Day was only half over. She would have to think up a little something for Sal.

It was April Fools' Day on Orthopedic Ward too. Cherry saw the debris of it as she reported on that afternoon: some crumpled telegrams which looked almost authentic, a package of dog biscuit (in a corner with tissue paper and ribbon, where someone had disgustedly hurled the gift), and a crutch with a string of garlic tied on it. Not much like a hospital, this cheerful, noisy place with bathrobed patients wandering around, kidding and entertaining themselves. Cherry passed a knot of them in the bright corridor outside the ward. There were man-sized couches out here, under a window wall, and a radio, a piano, a table littered with magazines and books, a ping-pong table too. All the young men looked—and actually were—so strong, young, solid, healthy, despite bandaged arms and legs. One embarrassed lad was being visited by parents who anxiously offered him brown paper bags of food.

Cherry grinned and went into the ward itself. She signed in—it was about one-thirty—and said good afternoon to the youthful nurse-lieutenant who was in charge of Orthopedic Ward.

"The patients have had their noon dinner, Lieutenant Ames. Will you just see who wants to nap and who would like something to do? I'll go off for my own lunch now, and then to a lecture. If the Ward Officer comes before I get back, there are some dressings to change. Edith Randall is working in the lab next door if you want help."

Cherry was pleased to be left in charge here. She would have a visit with Jim Travers and her original little group. Afternoons on the wards were always leisurely and pleasant. Orthopedic was an "active" ward with many of the patients up, only nine or ten in bed. A dozen of the almost-well patients were strolling in now after having spent busy mornings in the crafts shops of the hospital.

Cherry went over to say hello to Jim. He was in bed. Like all new arrivals, he had been X-rayed, thoroughly checked up, and given his beginning treatments. Four or five days ago, Jim had had a further operation. Now the stump of his leg was draining.

"Hello, how d'you feel?" Cherry greeted him. "You look pretty good today."

"I feel pretty good, thanks. How are you?"

Cherry called over a medical Wac to refill the crushed ice bag for Jim's leg. She straightened his rubber draw sheet and raised the head of his bed slightly. Then she told him:

"I'm coming back to you after I tend to the rest of the fellows."

Jim smiled wanly. "Going to work on my morale?"

"No pep talks," Cherry promised. "No phony rays of sunshine. I have a niftier plan."

"What?"

"Won't tell you."

"Isn't she a pest?"

That came from the next bed, from Bailey Matthews lying flat in his body length cast.

Cherry gave his red hair a tug. "Ah, good day to you, Brother Turtle. If you'd just pull your head down inside that shell, I wouldn't have to listen to your insults."

The Texan looked disgusted. "I wish everybody'd stop being so doggone *nice* to me. I can't stand it. Those Red Cross females—I have to lie here flat on my back while they *do good* to me!"

Cherry ignored this ungracious gripe. "How'd you like to read?"

"Me? With a book? Do I look high-brow to you?"

"A book about horses. Mostly pictures. Different breeds and all. You can have comic strips too."

"Well, that's different. But you know I can't read in this position!"

"Read on the ceiling," Cherry said airily.

"Now I know you're crazy!" Matty exploded.

But Cherry fixed him up. She brought a little machine resembling the home-style still pictures projector, set it on the floor, and put a cord with a push button in his hand. Then she inserted a 35-mm. microfilm into the projector. Hy Leader in his wheel chair and Ralph Pernatelli came up to watch. Jim looked on, too.

"Press the button, Matty," she said. She drew down a window shade behind him.

The machine's light turned on and page one, saying "Ride 'Em, Cowboy!" with a picture of a galloping horse, appeared two feet long on the ceiling, over Matty's astonished eyes.

"Well, I'll be doggoned!" Hy Leader said. He nearly fell out of his wheel chair trying to tilt it back so he too could lie flat and read. Cherry started to adjust the chair back for him. "I'll do it myself," he protested, and did.

Ralph lay down flat on the floor.

Matty finally reacted. "It's not bad at all," he begrudged. He looked perfectly delighted.

"Press the button to turn the page," Cherry said. But they had forgotten she existed. Cherry chuckled to herself. Matty stopped his griping, Hy and Ralph forgot their throbbing pain, even Jim showed some interest, the moment they had something to keep them busy. "I guess that's the whole secret," she thought. She went along down the row of beds.

The teacher, George Blumenthal, was sitting up in bed. He was laboriously trying to write with his left hand.

"Stout fella," Cherry said.

George looked up and smiled rather shyly. "It was my wife's idea. She said on the phone to try it."

Cherry hoped other patients' families would take such constructive attitudes. She had a look at his dressing, then wheeled over the dressing carriage, took off the stained dressing with phenol forceps, and put on new sterile gauze with sterile forceps.

"Sorry to interrupt your writing, teacher, but we don't allow infections around here."

"Wait. I want to show you something." He fumbled under his pillow. "These are pictures of my wife and baby. I've never seen the baby. She was born while I was overseas fighting."

"They're darlings, both of them," Cherry said warmly, looking at the pictures.

"The baby's name is Barbara Ann." George Blumenthal proudly put the pictures away. "I hope the doctors won't keep me here long."

The patient in the next bed, Cherry knew, had no such impetus to get well quickly. This fretful, sulky boy felt sorry for himself. In fact, Cherry suspected that he enjoyed self-pity. And his low spirits were retarding his recovery.

"Hi, Orphan," she greeted him. "When are you going to get up and take a stroll down the hall? How about right now?"

"What have I got to get up for?" he mumbled.

Two young men playing cards on the next bed jeered, "Poor Joe, nobody loves him."

"Who could love a growler? Ah, pipe down, Joe. You should see *my* relatives. You'd be glad you're an orphan."

Cherry concealed her amusement at the way the lads themselves took care of a griper. "Come on, Joe, get up. You're well enough. This is an order."

He pointed to the letters on the pocket of his bathrobe, MDUSA, which stood for Medical Department, United States Army.

"See that?" he said gloomily. "Many die, you shall also."

"I've seen you eat," Cherry said. "You won't die, not with that appetite. Get up, now, Orphan."

She hurried him along a bit, for she really did have a plan about Jim Travers for this afternoon. With all the speed of a lazy cow, Joe climbed out of the high white iron bed, found his shoes, and clumped off wearing an injured air. Two minutes later, Cherry glimpsed him in the corridor. He was carefully setting the classic April Fools' trap, tying a long string to a purse, then leaving the purse to be "found."

Cherry saw to others of the patients: one with his leg held aloft in traction, listening to his radio, who matter-of-factly displayed the shell splinter on his bedside table—two Army fliers, making model planes, to exercise their wounded arms and shoulders—a lad who said he tried to take a nap "but it's too noisy and party-like in here." By midafternoon Red Cross Gray Ladies came in and passed out supplies of wool and leather to work with. Then corpsmen brought trays of ice cream and cake, with the compliments of the hospital chaplains. Finally the chief nurse of the ward returned and Cherry made her report.

Now she went back to Jim. Cherry felt he needed extra help, for in many ways—his severe wound, his elderly mother, his gentle nature—Jim was worse off than these other men.

"Think you could manage a ride in a chair, Jim?"

He said he had already been out of bed yesterday.

"All right, then. There's something you ought to see."

"It's no use, ma'am," the young man said. "I'll get well and all but—" His lips tightened. He had no real hope. Though he must once have been a spunky sort, his confidence in himself now was gone. He had not yet, Cherry knew, faced the ordeal of telling his mother.

He cooperated well enough, though, as Cherry had two corpsmen lift him into a wheel chair. She settled him with ice bag and blankets, thinking, "Jim's so sweet and decent, he'll cooperate even when he doesn't want to." Her respect for him increased still more when she saw how erect and soldierly he sat in the wheel chair.

She wheeled him down the corridor to an elevator, then downstairs, then out the lobby into the wooden covered walk. It was pleasant being half indoors, half out, with the branches of trees trailing on the wooden roof.

"Anyone play any tricks on you today?" she teased as she rolled him along.

"No one but you, ma'am. What are we going to see?"

A strange gymnasium was what they had come to see. Here physical therapists, men in Army uniform, worked one by one with the patients. Here was a patient in pajamas laboriously turning a wheel with his braced arm. Another, with a leather-and-steel leg, slowly practiced standing, then taking a step, inside what looked like an adult-sized playpen. Still another with a leather leg held on to a handrail on the wall and walked. The determination on their faces was heartbreaking and magnificent to see.

Cherry moved slightly so that she could see Jim's face. He was staring.

"Anyone with a leg that doesn't fit?" one of the physical therapists called out to the room in general.

"I have a leg that doesn't work!" the patient in the pen shouted back.

There was general laughter. Cherry saw Jim's mouth tremble, as if he would almost smile with them.

"All sorts of interesting equipment here," said Cherry casually. She pointed out a strapping soldier lying under a heat lamp. Another worked a foot press. One big fellow near them patiently groped to pick up pebbles with his toes.

"I caught a bullet in the Huertgen Forest," he called over to Jim. "This leg was pretty useless at first."

Jim echoed faintly, "At first."

They stayed awhile longer. Then Cherry saw that her patient was growing tired. She wheeled him toward the door, but before they left, the patient who had been slowly walking along the wall hurried toward them on crutches.

"Hello," he said to Jim. "I see you're where I was, a few weeks ago. They had to amputate my left leg and I thought I would never walk or make a living for my family again."

"Yeah," said Jim but he was listening hard.

"Well, I was wrong. Everything is changed now."

"I see. Thanks a lot."

"Sure, fellow. They've got a car here, fixed with special pedals and brakes so we can drive. Those cars are going to be on the market right along."

Jim did not say a word on their way back to the ward. Neither did Cherry.

When she was helping him back into bed, Jim said:

"I think I'd like to phone my mother."

Cherry went off duty feeling very happy indeed.

Next, she hunted up Sal Steen and found her, head dripping, in the beauty parlor in Nurses' Quarters. Cherry told Sal that she had duly secured the six grams of tetrathyazide from Nephalogy and that Lieutenant Lewis on 2D2 had been most grateful to receive it. Sal could only mutter a mystified "Thanks so much."

Finally, Cherry went up to Sal's room, made a pie-bed, systematically turned all Sal's clothes wrong side out, and knotted her shoe laces.

All in all, Cherry considered as she went down to dinner, she had had an eminently satisfactory April Fools' Day.

CHAPTER V

A Little Boy

CHERRY HAD HEARD VAGUELY ABOUT MR. AND MRS. DEmarest. They were well-to-do people who lived near Graham Hospital, in a big house with a rambling estate. Part of their home, and their gardens, were always hospitably open to convalescing soldiers from Graham, to drop in whenever they pleased. Cherry gathered that the Demarests were very pleasant and well liked. She heard too something less happy: that they had an only child, a son of four or five, who was very sick.

It remained for Sal to say to Cherry late one afternoon, after they had both gone off duty:

"Would you risk having your heart broken?"

"Why, Sal, that doesn't sound like you!"

"This is nothing to laugh about. But I would like you to meet some awfully nice people—the Demarests."

"The Demarests! I would like to know them. When?"

"Right now. We'll get our coats."

"But shouldn't we change into fresh uniforms? They're probably older people—sort of formal—they'd expect us to look just so—"

"Nothing of the sort. Come along."

Sal and Cherry took the bus at the hospital gate, after showing the MP their credentials, and rode to the village. From there, they walked two blocks to the Demarest grounds. They entered a series of gardens and lawns, and walked almost another two blocks, until a stately house loomed up before them. It was a large, formal house and a butler opened the door. The two girls stepped into a circular hallway.

"Good afternoon, Lieutenant Steen," the butler said. "Mrs. Demarest is expecting you." He took their coats and asked Cherry's name, then led them to an open door.

"Lieutenant Steen, Lieutenant Ames," he said, and withdrew.

A pretty, youngish woman rose from a group of hospital people having tea. She came over to them smiling, hand outstretched.

"Hello, Sal, I saved you some muffins. And you, Lieutenant—"

"Cherry Ames, Mrs. Demarest," Sal introduced them.

"Cherry—that's an appropriate name for you. I'm glad Sal brought you. Mr. Demarest and I would like

A LITTLE BOY

to know all the Graham people. Come in and have tea."

Mrs. Demarest settled the girls on a sofa, introduced them to the dozen convalescing soldiers and their three nurses, and served them tea and sandwiches from a well-laden little table. While the soldiers engaged their hostess in conversation, Cherry took a moment to study her.

Young Mrs. Demarest was one of the most appealing women Cherry had ever seen. Not precisely pretty, she had an expression of responsiveness that made her glow like a lighted lamp. That warmth was in her face, her voice, her eyes, her eager movements. She was slender, brown-haired, and dressed very simply in a dark-green knitted suit.

The room caught Cherry's eye next. It was a vast, beautiful sitting room, yellow and white, with fine polished furniture, mirrors, endless lamps and bibelots, Oriental rugs glowing like stained-glass windows on the floor. The room was formal, but the people living here were not.

Mrs. Demarest came to sit with Sal and Cherry.

"How did the boy with the bad back come through his operation?" she asked Sal. She listened with real concern to Sal's reply, then said, "Is there anything he'd like that we could send him?"

"Yes," said Sal frankly. "He's longing for books about Asia. He was stationed in India and in Burma, and wants to know more about that whole part of the world. There isn't much on that subject in our hospital library."

Mrs. Demarest took a tiny notebook from her pocket and made an entry. Cherry saw there were many entries in that little book.

"Thank you, Mrs. Demarest," Sal said. "He'll enjoy them."

"It's little enough, my dear. What about your patients, Lieutenant Ames? Won't you tell me about them?—Oh, wait a moment. Here comes my husband. I know he'll want to hear too."

A stocky, smiling young man walked in. He had very blue eyes and, like his wife, real cordiality. He spoke to all the visitors, seemed to know everyone already. His wife called him over and introduced him to Cherry.

"Hello, Miss Cherry. I hope you'll come often, and bring your soldier patients."

His handshake was firm and warm. Cherry thanked him and promised to bring her charges when they were better.

Then there was a moment's silence while Mrs. Demarest looked anxiously at her husband.

"What did the New York specialist say?"

"He said no."

An expression of sadness permeated both their faces—such sadness that Cherry was distressed herself. For in that sadness was hopelessness.

"How—how is Toby?" Mrs. Demarest faltered. "I haven't been upstairs this past hour."

"Just as well, Grace. Toby is resting. And all these young people take our minds off our trouble."

Cherry glanced questioningly at Sal. Sal's face was stony. Mrs. Demarest noticed the glance and explained quite simply:

"We have a little boy, four years old, who has an incurable illness. At least, the doctors know of no cure. Toby has been sick quite a long time... You see, Lieutenant Cherry, Toby's system cannot absorb food. He gets no nourishment at all out of the good food we feed him. So he's—he's starving." She bit her lip. Her eyes were suspiciously bright. "He's wasting away."

"Starving in the midst of plenty," young Mr. Demarest said quietly. "And there's nothing anyone can do."

Cherry was horrified. "Aren't there intravenous foods, or vitamins, or medicines, that can nourish him?" she asked. "Or a corrective medicine?"

"Nothing," Mr. Demarest said. "Toby cannot absorb anything at all. Or if there is something, we haven't found it so far. We have a dozen eminent doctors on the case but—" He shook his head.

Cherry felt their helplessness as if a pile of bricks had dropped on her heart. No words could express her concern: she simply looked at these two stricken people.

Mrs. Demarest smiled wanly at Cherry. "He's grown too weak and thin even to play any more. He has to stay in bed all the time."

Sal blew her nose and looked away.

"I wish I could see him," Cherry breathed. "He must be a lonely little boy. And I—love children."

"It might do him good," Toby's father agreed. "We haven't given up hope by any means." He said it with bravado.

As Cherry and Sal followed Mr. Demarest upstairs, Sal whispered to Cherry:

"They must like you. They let very few people see the child."

When a trained nurse opened the door into a nursery, Cherry understood why. The tiny boy propped up in the bed was more like a ghost, a dying doll, than a real flesh-and-blood child.

He opened exhausted blue eyes, blue as his father's, and looked up at the three adults standing around his bed. Cherry saw the four-year-old's tiny bony wrists, the scrawny little neck, the hollows in his temples. Beside his hand lay a toy duck but the little fellow was too tired to play with it.

"Hello, son," his father said softly. "Here are two nurses who take care of sick soldiers. Even soldiers get sick, too, you know."

Cherry and Sal said hello in unison. Little Toby stared soberly at them.

"Where are the soldiers?"

"In bed like you," Sal said.

"But the soldiers are getting well and so will you," Cherry said.

He sighed, a breath of a sigh, and smiled. It was an oddly grave smile for such a little face.

"Would you like to hear a story?" Cherry asked gently, looking at the unused toys around the beautifully appointed nursery. She glanced at Mr. Demarest for permission. "I'll take less than five minutes."

"A story?" Toby whispered. "Which story?"

"One you probably never heard before." Cherry sat down beside his bed and took Toby's hand. It was a pathetic scrap of a hand. "Once upon a time there was a man named Rip Van Winkle. He had a nice dog, named Wolf, and a very mean wife." She looked into the boy's blue eyes as she retold the tale. Those eyes grew full of wonder.

"And would you believe it, poor Rip had slept *twenty years!*" Cherry finished. "But his old dog Wolf, and all the townspeople, finally remembered Rip. Now when you hear thunder, Toby, you'll know it's the old Dutch men throwing balls along the mountains."

His face was bright with interest.

"When's it going to be thunder?"

"Next time it rains. You listen for the thunder."

"And Rip was happy ever after?"

"Yes, Rip lived to a ripe old age."

"Now tell me a nuther story."

"Next time," Cherry promised. His gaze followed her longingly as she rose.

"I hope there will be a next time," Mr. Demarest said, as he softly closed Toby's door behind them. "I really think Toby will be waiting for you and your next story."

Downstairs, he told his wife about their visit to Toby. "He's always so listless but, Grace, you should have seen how interested he was!"

Mrs. Demarest turned to Cherry. "Will you be Toby's Scheherazade? We tell him stories too but perhaps he is too used to us. And if he has something to look forward to—something to I—" She checked herself. "Something to keep him going, I mean."

Cherry knew Mrs. Demarest had started to say, "Something to live for." Something to feed his spirit, or call it his interest and his will, which might keep alive his starving little body. Even a four-year-old, Cherry knew, might be sustained through imagination and love.

"I'll come back as often as I have free time," she promised soberly.

The gratitude in their two faces made her feel very humble indeed.

It was easier said than done, to go back to the Demarests' often. Cherry's work was heavy, and her first duty was to her soldier patients. But she had an obligation to that pathetic child, too. It weighed on her when three, four, and then five days slipped by, and she did not get over there. The picture of Toby slowly wasting away, while parents, doctors, nurses stood by helpless, haunted Cherry. Never in all her nursing experience had she run across a patient so appealing and so doomed.

"And anyhow," Cherry said to Sal, in Cherry's room one night, "suppose my storytelling doesn't work? Doesn't continue to hold his interest?"

"You're a great worrier," Sal said laconically. "Ten to one it at least helps." She scowled. "What's on my mind is the doctors on that case. Why don't they *do* something?"

"A very nice, unreasonable speech, Miss Steen."

"All right, now we've both bawled each other out." Sal and Cherry grinned at each other in mutual understanding. "Ames, you show up at the Demarests' tomorrow with a story, or else."

"But I have late duty tomorrow."

"I'll go on duty for you. Fix it with my supervisor."

So Cherry was ushered once again into the quiet nursery, this time by Grace Demarest. The little boy's pinched face lighted, and he struggled to sit up.

"Toby's really glad to see you," his mother said to Cherry happily.

"I like you, Cherry," Toby announced.

Cherry sat down by his bedside and started to tell him the Victorian fairy tale of the golden statue which had eyes of ruby and a living heart, and the sparrow which flew to do the statue's bidding. But she had forgotten one thing. Toby was fumbling for her hand, as part of their already regular ceremony.

"—so finally the stupid mayor had the statue taken down, and melted, and the little sparrow flew away," Cherry finished. "But many, many people remembered them both, to this very day."

Toby heaved a big sigh. "Poor statue. Poor sparrow. If I was there, I'd 'uv brung them home with me." His cheeks were faintly flushed with satisfaction. "Now tell me a nuther story."

But the precious five minutes were up. As Cherry stood up to leave, the little boy still clung to her hand.

"I'll tell *you* a story," he pleaded. "'Bout a statue."

"Next time, dear," Cherry said. "Don't forget the sparrow. He was quite a brave bird, wasn't he?"

"I won't forget," he promised. "When you comin' again, Cherry?"

That was the little cry which followed her through busy days: "When are you comin' back to me?" She did her very best to get there often. And as she continued to go and spin tales, the dying little boy grew more and more attached to Cherry.

She came to know and care for the child, and for his parents too. She appreciated fully now the generosity and the pathos of this beautiful house. She marveled at the way young Mr. and Mrs. Demarest steeled themselves, showing only a happy face to the soldier

A LITTLE BOY

visitors. It was as if, unable to help their own son, they were determined to help other people's sons out of the despondency of illness.

Mrs. Demarest said to Cherry late one afternoon when she insisted Cherry remain after the storytelling for tea in her own room:

"I read of a woman who years ago lost her only child. She must be a sensible woman. Instead of grieving over one baby, she went out and collected all the orphan babies she could find, all over the country, and then she found good homes for them. She's been doing that for thirty years, and she says she's had thousands of babies instead of just one. Maybe—maybe I'll do something like that."

Cherry put aside her cup and saucer to say earnestly, "But you mustn't give up hope, Mrs. Demarest. You never can tell about these things. There always is a chance."

"The doctors don't seem to think so. In fact, some of them talk of withdrawing from the case, because they feel there is nothing they can do for us."

Cherry inquired exactly who was treating Toby. Mrs. Demarest named several eminent physicians and specialists.

"And Dr. Orchard, our local doctor," she added. "I'd like you to meet him. You've never been here when he has called, but I believe he's downstairs now. Let's go down and see, shall we?"

In the big sitting room, Mr. Demarest was entertaining convalescing soldiers. A few civilians were here today too, including a young man whom Mrs. Demarest beckoned over.

"Dr. Orchard, Lieutenant Ames."

Dr. Orchard was short and plump and very sure of himself for such a young man. His round fair face was shrewd, almost cold. However, his manner seemed pleasant enough as he talked with Cherry about her work at the Army hospital and his private practice here in the village.

"Dr. Orchard takes care of my son Toby," Mrs. Demarest told Cherry.

"Oh, I'm only one of several consulting doctors for Toby," Dr. Orchard said, but there was no modesty in the way he said it.

"You're the baby among all those famous specialists," Mrs. Demarest smiled. "Even if they leave us in the lurch, I know *you* won't."

"My dear Mrs. Demarest," Dr. Orchard smiled unctuously at her. "Never fear! I could never leave so charming a woman in the lurch."

Cherry winced at his ingratiating tones. She wondered how the Demarests, who could afford the best doctors, had happened to choose this young local doctor. No doubt Dr. Orchard was competent. It certainly was quite a feather in his cap—quite a boost to his beginning career—to be called in along with famous practitioners. How had he managed it? Perhaps simply because the Demarests knew him? Or with that ingratiating manner of his?

"I don't like him," Cherry thought later. "There's something about him that's not quite sincere—Oh, but I shouldn't be making snap judgments about Dr. Orchard on the basis of one little meeting," she reprimanded herself.

And Cherry continued faithfully to go to the Demarests' and sit holding Toby's hand, recounting fabulous legends about the elves who lived in tree trunks and fashioned a magic mirror, the winged steed that raced with the sun, the mermaid who loved a human prince and suffered for it.

And Toby listened blissfully, begging for more, while daily he became thinner, weaker, a shadow of a child, receding into a world of shadows.

If only they could snatch him back!

CHAPTER VI

Midge's Big Romance

IT WAS SUNDAY MORNING. CHERRY WOKE UP AND BLINKED at her own red-and-white room in Hilton. For a moment she thought, "This is too good to be true." Then she remembered riding the interurban trolley over from the hospital, Saturday evening. Cherry sniffed and listened. From downstairs came her parents' voices and the aroma of buttermilk pancakes for a Sunday morning treat. Church bells were ringing two blocks away.

Cherry staggered to her side window and leaned out over the top of the high lilac bush. It was a heavenly day—a fine blue sky—millions of cloud-islands scudding before the wind—earth and air smelling fragrant. "It's spring," she promised herself. "And I'm home!"

Being home was still an unaccustomed luxury. Cherry soaked herself leisurely in the bathtub, then donned her most frivolous underthings though she still

MIDGE'S BIG ROMANCE 69

had to wear her khaki uniform. She dawdled over breakfast, cooked by her mother. Velva had gone home for Sunday. She even demanded black olives along with the pancakes—and got them.

"It's still such a novelty to you," she teased her parents, "having me home, that I could ask you for an ermine coat and probably get it."

"You could not," said her father. "But as a mark of my esteem, I'll let you have the funnies." He handed her the bright-hued pages across the table and poured himself another cup of coffee.

"Will," said Mrs. Ames ruefully, "that's your fifth cup. You know you always feel dreadful on Mondays—after all that coffee."

"I feel like an old inner tube on Mondays," Mr. Ames admitted cheerfully. He passed Cherry the pancakes again. "You have to eat your brother's share for him, since he's not here."

"I expect Charlie would do as much for me," Cherry agreed, and started in on another stack. "Mother, what are you looking so preoccupied about? Charlie can take care of himself."

Mrs. Ames rested her pretty face in her hands. "I'm not worried about Charles. It's Midge and Dr. Joe I'm concerned about. Midge is having a big romance. Today is *the* day, I gather. And it—Well, that child's antics are simply indescribable. Perhaps you'd better stop by at the Fortunes' house, Cherry. Midge does listen to you."

"Yes, see what advice you can give to the lovelorn," her father grinned.

This was the first Cherry had heard of Midge's romance. Surprised and rather amused, she strolled along the quiet Sunday streets. She enjoyed seeing all the familiar places again: the stately pillared Pendleton house on the corner, set far back in its long sweep of lawn—the rather grim, gabled stone house which Cherry as a child had thought must be haunted because it looked so forbidding—the brick high school where she had had both good and bad hours. Several old friends waved to her along the way to the Fortunes' small white cottage.

One of Cherry's long-time daydreams was to take this neglected cottage in hand, for someone could make it lovely. Looking like a dollhouse (though actually it was roomy inside), the cottage cried out for a fresh coat of white paint and latticed roses around the door. The weeds should be pulled too, and flowers planted instead, along the flagstone path Cherry trod now.

Apparently Midge had the same idea, only applied to the interior of the cottage. Midge, with her hair strained back in pin curls, opened the front door, and an overpowering fragrance of lilacs practically smote Cherry down.

"Midge! Is this a funeral parlor? Or are you planning to anesthetize somebody? I can't breathe in here!"

The living room was crammed to overflowing with purple lilacs. On the tables, on the floor beside the sofa, at the window, in vases, jars, jugs, even in a bucket, branches of nodding lilac left almost no space to turn around in. It was lovely enough in a startling way.

"It's a bower," Midge said aggrievedly. "You seem to have no artistic appreciation. Anybody'd know this is good psychology, too. I've got a caller coming this afternoon at five, you see," Midge explained importantly. "The lilacs are to put Tom in a romantic mood."

"I hope Tom likes flowers." Cherry choked a little in the sickening sweetness. She ran a finger over the dusty table top. "Shall I draw a heart?" she suggested. "What's Tom's last initial?"

"All right," Midge sputtered. "I'll dust."

She marched off in high dudgeon, straight into an overhanging branch of lilac. It left a wide smear of pollen on her flushed young face.

Cherry knocked on a door off the living room. "Dr. Joe! Good morning!"

He opened the door into his homemade laboratory. "Thank heavens you came over! Midge is driving me to distraction." He sat down wearily on a high wooden stool and put his hands in the pockets of his white lab coat. "She drives me out of every room and says I mustn't brew any chemicals today. Seems it would interfere with those blasted lilacs."

Cherry could not help giggling. Dr. Joe looked so harassed, bewilderment all over his seamed face. "Listen!" he said disgustedly.

72 *CHERRY AMES, VETERANS' NURSE*

Cherry listened. From the living room came a phonograph record playing, slow, sad, sirupy sweet. A tenor voice bleated, "Do you love me—will you love me—"

"She's been playing that danged record day and night. Midge!" Dr. Joe lifted his deep voice. "I can't stand much more! Please shut that thing off!"

"—morning, noon, and night—you are my heart's delight—" the record groaned on. Cherry ran into the deserted living room. "—when will you see the light—" Cherry stopped the tenor's sufferings at that point. There was a sigh from Dr. Joe, and a yell from Midge in the vicinity of the kitchen.

Cherry found her anxiously stirring at the stove.

"Fudge," she explained, wiping her perspiring forehead with the back of her hand. "For Tom."

"Who is this Tom anyway?"

"Tell you later when you help me with my dress. You *will* help me, won't you? Be a dear and beat this fudge while I ice the cake."

"Did you dust?"

"Oh, Tom will never notice a little dust."

Cherry stirred, Midge spread chocolate icing and then licked the icing bowl.

"Perhaps," Cherry suggested as tactfully as she could, "perhaps Tom would like to do some of the providing himself. Perhaps he'll be a little embarrassed or scared off by all this militant preparation. Sweetie, aren't you overdoing things just a bit? Why don't you—ah—give *him* a chance to do something for *you*? Say, buy you a soda on this date?"

"It's not a date." Midge's luminous hazel eyes flew open. "It's a business appointment. Now pour out the fudge and we'll see about the dress. I'll make the hot chocolate when he comes."

Cherry did not press her point. If Midge was determined to drown Tom in chocolate and suffocate him in lilacs that was Midge's business. Tom would have to fend for himself.

In Midge's topsy-turvy bedroom, Cherry cleared aside a pile of clothes on the bed, put the shoes on the floor, and sat down. "This room looks as if a cyclone had struck it."

Midge pawed through a drawer searching for face cream. "I feel like a cyclone hit *me*," she confided. "Now here's the dress—" She dived into the closet, but Cherry interrupted.

"First tell me about this 'business' appointment. Who is this dream man of yours?"

"Tom Heaton," Midge said breathlessly. "He's not mine—*yet*. He's been in my class all along, for years and years practically, but I just realized this week that I'm in love with him. I realized it when I knew he was *coming here-alone*! Because the Student Organization assigned Tom and me as a committee of two. We have to study the lunchroom situation and make a report."

"What's the matter with the lunchroom? No lunch?"

"Oh, Cherry, this love was destined to be! Tom is so handsome. Such a gentleman. He hasn't noticed me yet—romantically, I mean—but I've always admired him. All the girls think he's tops. That good-looking Miller girl thinks she owns Tom but *I'll*—"

"Whoa! You mean Tom is coming here in all innocence to discuss—"

"—and here's the creation!"

Midge whirled into the closet and came up with a creation indeed. It was ruffled rosy faille, made by Midge herself and not made very well. Cherry examined it and forbore saying her young friend would look like a comic valentine in it.

"Midge, this isn't exactly your style, is it? You're such a tomboy—you look so sort of dashing in sports clothes—" Cherry struggled. "Wouldn't your yellow flannel and gold jewelry be more becoming?"

"But Grace Miller wore a dress like this to the school dance and Tom danced three times with her!" Midge wailed.

Cherry pointed out that that was at an evening dance. That Grace Miller was tiny and blonde, while Midge was tall and willowy and of tawny coloring. That Grace's father and Tom's father were in business together, and Tom probably had had strict instructions from his parents not to neglect Grace. That, besides, this fussy dress was a mess.

"All right, the yellow flannel," Midge said bravely, and she hung the creation away.

"I'll lend you my best perfume," Cherry comforted her. "I'll go home, have dinner, and come back here with the perfume around four."

"No! Please come back practically instantly! I have to rehearse the conversation with you."

"How can you rehearse a—"

"Cherry, I *need* you! This afternoon is a crisis in my life!"

Back in her own house, Cherry entertained her parents with an account of Midge's "crisis." Mr. and Mrs. Ames thought it hilarious but Cherry sympathized with Midge's efforts. She was only afraid that Midge was going about it too obviously.

Cherry lingered after dinner to visit with her parents. She hoped they would not mind her spending the afternoon at the Fortunes' instead of at home. After all, she could be home almost every Sunday, or whatever free day she had.

"Go right ahead, dear," her mother said. "I hope *you* won't mind when I tell you Dad and I have already accepted an invitation for this evening. But I'm leaving a nice buffet supper for you in the icebox. I'd suggest you bring Dr. Joe and Midge here for supper too. That poor man isn't thriving on Midge's cooking. Something will have to be done about him, if his health is to improve."

Cherry thought, walking back to the Fortunes' cottage with the perfume, that doing something about Midge might be the first step in helping Dr. Joe relax.

76 *CHERRY AMES, VETERANS' NURSE*

That mournful record was playing again when Cherry entered. She turned it off, and set to work dusting the living room, ducking lilacs as she went. Dr. Joe told her that Midge had given him lunch, of a sort. Cherry coaxed him to take a nap, in his room off the laboratory.

"You won't be safe anywhere except in your own room," she warned him. "Not until after Tom has come and gone."

Dr. Joe holed in with books, and the Sunday newspaper. "It's hard being a father," he said plaintively.

Cherry found Midge in a state of wild nervousness. She had brushed out her fluffy, light-brown hair over her shoulders and was battling to wind it into curls.

"But why not wear it loose and flowing, as you always do?" Cherry inquired. "Don't you want Tom to recognize you?"

"I want Tom to think I'm pretty"— she flung the hairbrush on the floor and started all over with a comb— "not just that little brat at school!"

"You'd better look and act natural," Cherry said dryly. "No use trying to be a third-rate movie queen."

"If you aren't going to be any more help than this, Cherry Ames, you can go away!"

Cherry forgave her her crossness, for Midge's hands were actually shaking. Cherry set the perfume down on the dresser.

"Mmm, thanks. Cherry, what do you think of this? I could ask Tom to keep my compact in his pocket—and then I could forget to ask him for it back—and then he'd *have* to come over again to return it to me! Slick?"

Cherry perched on the foot of the bed and swung her legs. "It's full of ifs and maybes. No, madam. If you want Tom to come again, don't trick him into it. He'd resent it. Be so nice he'll *want* to see you again." She thought of her father's face when he had said "advice to the lovelorn" this morning and she shook inwardly with laughter. But Midge's upturned, anxious face was nothing to laugh at.

"How can I make him like me?" Midge said very humbly and pathetically.

"By being yourself. Your very nicest self."

"But—but—s'pose I do, and then he doesn't like me?" Midge quavered.

Cherry bent and patted Midge's cheek. "That would only mean that you and Tom weren't a good combination. Then you'd find another boy. Stop being so *desperate*. Anyhow, I'll bet Tom will like you just fine!"

Midge brightened. Cherry examined her sticky fingers. Midge's face was smeared with face cream. "Hand me that tissue," Cherry sighed and resigned herself for the rest of the afternoon, while Midge went over and over what she would say and do at the fatal hour of five.

Shortly before five, Cherry prepared to leave. She was going into Dr. Joe's laboratory, to invite him and Midge to supper, when the doorbell rang.

"Cherry, go to the door!" Midge shrieked. "I haven't got my jewelry on!"

Cherry obediently retraced her steps through the bower of lilacs, now slightly wilted, and opened the front door.

A pleasant-looking boy stood on the step.

"I'm Tom Heaton," he said. "Is Midge in?"

"Yes, Midge is expecting you," Cherry answered, and that was a masterpiece of understatement. "Come in. I'm her friend, Cherry Ames."

She led him into the living room and they found seats among the lilacs. If Tom was surprised by the purple profusion, he was too well-bred to show it. Cherry chatted with him for a few minutes about his family, whom she knew casually, and about what the high school was like now. Tom was a poised and impersonal boy, Cherry noted. She decided after close watch that he had probably not even noticed the lilacs. He merely seemed to find the room warm and stuffy.

Midge suddenly appeared in the doorway. She looked quite dazzling. Cherry at once excused herself, said she would just speak to Dr. Joe a moment, and then be going.

In the laboratory Dr. Joe was fiddling with slides and his microscope.

"He's here," Cherry whispered conspiratorially.

"What's he like?" Dr. Joe whispered back.

"Seems nice. He—"

Just then the key turned in the lock. Midge, wanting no intruders in the living room, had locked them in. There was no back door out from here, either.

Cherry laughed uncontrollably under her breath. "We're trapped in here!"

That was how she and Dr. Joe became unwilling witnesses—at least by sound effects.

First there was a loud masculine sneeze. Then came Midge's anxious murmur, followed by a whole volley of sneezes. For several minutes they heard tramping footsteps, heavy objects being moved, water swishing, all punctuated by sneezes.

"The boy is allergic to flowers," Dr. Joe figured out in a whisper. "They're moving the lilacs away."

"Oh, poor Midge!" Cherry gasped. "What next?"

Next came the opening bars of "Do you love me—can you love me—" Dr. Joe winced. The record played straight through. Then, for a long time, two earnest voices labored along. The only word Cherry could make out clearly was "lunchroom."

Cherry began to despair for Midge's romance. Then she and Dr. Joe heard a rattle of dishes. Apparently Midge, failing in her frontal attack, was now trying the gastronomical approach. As the dishes clattered, the two voices in the living room grew noticeably more cheerful.

Suddenly the phonograph burst forth into the hot classic, "Is You Is Or Is You Ain't My Baby?" The unmistakable crashes of jitterbugging shook the locked laboratory door. This violence went on for forty minutes, while Dr. Joe paced up and back like an angry tiger.

It was twilight when the front door slammed. A second later, the key turned in the lock and Midge released them. She leaned in the doorway, completely worn out.

"He *loves* to dance," she panted. "And he ate up every crumb of the refreshments! And he wants me to be his partner in the dance contest next month! Ohhhh!"

"Does he love you, can he love you, will he love you?" Dr. Joe grunted. He got up and stretched. "Is you is or is you not—Bah!"

"Good for you, Midge," Cherry said hastily. "Come over to my house now. It's late and your poor Dad needs his supper. You and I'll talk while we're getting it on the table."

At home, Cherry turned on all the lamps in the downstairs rooms. She urged Dr. Joe to rest in the big leather chair, in the softly lighted living room. The elderly man was tired after his all-day ordeal. But he asked Cherry to wait a moment, although Midge had already headed for the kitchen.

"My little girl is growing up, Cherry."

"We-ell, if you'd call fudge and jitterbugging grown up," Cherry answered.

"But a romance—her sudden, intense interest in a young man—"

"A high school boy," Cherry gently corrected.

Dr. Joe sighed. "No, my dear. Midge is growing up. I'm going to lose her one of these days. Of course I want her to—to—"

"Don't worry so far in advance." Yet Cherry did feel sympathy for Dr. Joe. He seemed quite bewildered at Midge's sudden maturing. He was trying pathetically to do or feel whatever was best for the girl. He looked very much alone.

"You rest now, Dr. Joe," Cherry said softly. "I'll call you to supper in a few minutes." She went on out to the kitchen.

In the big white kitchen Midge was helping, in her own fashion. She had taken the pickles out of the icebox and was sampling them.

"If you want to help," Cherry said, rescuing the pickles, "you might take that bowl of flowers off the dining-room table, please, so I can set it."

"In my good dress?"

"Very true. Well, make a pitcher of ice water."

"Might splash my dress."

"All right, slice this bread, lovebird."

But the lovebird stood dreamily and watched Cherry take cold cuts and potato salad from the icebox and arrange them on platters. Finally she said:

"Cherry, I'm so happy."

Cherry looked up and her black eyes softened. Her young friend did look very happy. "Well, hurray."

82   *CHERRY AMES, VETERANS' NURSE*

"Isn't he a darling?"

"Yes, he seems very nice." Cherry collected china and silver on a tray, and trotted into the dining room. Midge trailed after her.

"Isn't he handsome?"

"Yes, very. Get the napkins, will you?"

"And doesn't Tom have lovely manners?"

"Scrumptious. Three napkins, please. Napkins!"

Cherry got the napkins herself, then returned to the kitchen, made coffee, cut the cake.

"Get out the butter, Miss Fortune."

But Midge only picked off bits of icing and gazed into space. "Tom," she murmured, and sighed. Without warning, she bolted.

Cherry smiled to herself and went on working alone. Perhaps Midge was not too young to feel very seriously. Perhaps Midge possessed depths which Cherry had never seen. Perhaps Midge was to be—

The radio suddenly shrieking jazz knocked all such thoughts out of Cherry's head. She heard that familiar crashing, too, and Dr. Joe's loud protests. The neighbors would be protesting next! Cherry ran into the living room.

"Midge, what a racket! Please—"

"I was only practicing so I can dance in the contest with Tom."

"She was only driving me to perdition! Did I say grown up?"

"You don't want me to win the contest—and Tom!"

Cherry switched the radio off and tried to calm two ruffled people.

"Love is fine but it'll ruin both of you! Now, please, please, wait quietly. Everything's practically ready."

Cherry almost ran, getting bread and butter and water on the table, then decided hurriedly to heat some soup. There was a suspicious silence from the front rooms. When she went to call the Fortunes, no one stirred.

Dr. Joe was asleep in the big chair. Cherry hesitated. But he looked so exhausted she did not disturb him.

A creak from the porch swing told Midge's whereabouts.

"I have no appetite," Midge sighed from out of the shadows. "Food! How disgusting. Who could eat when they're all swoony with love?"

So Cherry left Midge alone too.

Cherry sat down to supper all alone. Then she noticed that she herself was yawning over her plate, really tired.

"Romance a la Midge! It certainly is wearing." With a grin she reflected, "Poor Tom Heaton. I only hope he has a strong constitution!"

CHAPTER VII

First Test

JIM WAS BETTER. IN FACT, ALL OF ORTHOPEDIC WARD HAD perked up. By nine o'clock this April morning, with sun and clouds playing tag outside with the wind, Cherry's patients were bathed, fed, and doing their exercises.

"*One*—two, three, four-and-a-*one*—two, three, four," chanted the Reconditioning Officer, a sergeant, from the middle of the room.

All around him, the wounded men were trying their best. The bedridden cases were raising their arms or legs where they lay—Jim and the two fliers. Even Matty prone in his body cast worked his arms. Hy Leader in his wheel chair stretched and puffed away. The ambulatory cases stood beside their beds and exercised—George Blumenthal and the Orphan, Ralph Pernatelli with his unwieldy arm cast. The boys seemed to like it, Cherry noticed. It visibly toned them up.

"Keeping count, Nurse?" the Reconditioning Officer called to Cherry.

She held up her chart and pencil. "I certainly am!"

Every soldier who did his Physical Therapy exercises earned four "birdies" a day for five days a week. A birdie was a caduceus with a P.T. on it. Twenty birdies—a week's exercising—earned a two-day pass. With this goal, and with the tonic of teamwork, the men worked away enthusiastically.

"Everybody earned four birdies today!" Cherry announced as the exercises were finished. She was proud of these men's stamina and spirit.

"Nice going," the Reconditioning Officer told the men. "I'll have you taking five-mile hikes sooner than you think. All right, play ball!"

The sergeant tossed a big light basketball to Hy Leader. Hy threw it at the Orphan, the Orphan sent it to George. George missed but ran after it and hit it across the aisle to Jim. Jim tossed it gently to Matty in the next bed. Matty hurled it down the room to Ralph, who fumbled but grabbed it. Back and forth between forty beds, the ball flew.

"Who won?" asked the young chief nurse of the ward, when the game of volleyball was over. "Lieutenant Ames, please get the fellows ready now for Occupational Therapy." She herself went on writing out charts and reports.

Cherry, aided by a medical Wac and a very young girl assistant, went around the ward. She insisted that the patients lie down and rest quietly for ten minutes after their exercise. Then they all were given milk and a quick look-over to see that they were all right. The advanced patients went off to the crafts shops to work.

Now the Occupational Therapy instructor came in. She was a pleasant, firm person in Army uniform and highly trained. Coming along to help were two Red Cross ladies, in gray dresses and floating gray veils, carrying big boxes of supplies.

"Good morning!" said the O.T. officer. "Ready to work?"

The patients sat up and accepted the materials distributed. Only a few were enthusiastic, and a few were resigned—but all were determined. For though no one felt a burning interest in making thonged leather wallets or weaving a bath rug, these activities reconditioned injured muscles and helped the men get well.

"I have something new this morning," said the Occupational Therapist. "A factory owner near by offers to hire those of you able to make small radio parts. You'll be paid for the work, of course. A man from the radio factory is on his way to show you how. Who wants to try?"

A clamor went up. Everyone wanted to earn and be self-reliant. Not all, however, were yet healed enough to tie together these tiny wires and screws and spools.

There were disappointed faces—mutterings of "Well, by next month I'll be able!" And they fell to work on the knitting needles and printing blocks with a vengeance. "At least we won't lie around like vegetables!"

For the next hour the ward was a busy, comparatively quiet room. Cherry like the other nurses helped the patients, carrying out the instructions of the O.T. instructor. Cherry took Ralph Pernatelli's stiffened hand, which extended from his plaster cast, and gently fitted it around modeling clay. Then she moved her own hand over his into the clay.

"I want to make a—a rose. Oh! Say!"

"Hurt you, Ralph? The doctor prescribed this for you, you know."

"'S all right. Give me a minute, will you please?— Now let's try again."

Cherry's hand over his gently massaged and pushed. The clay took crude form.

"I get it," Ralph said with satisfaction. "This is going to be a masterpiece. Maybe I could do a portrait head later on, though."

Cherry again worked his hand on the clay for several minutes. Then he painfully, slowly, tried it himself. Beads of sweat stood out on Ralph's forehead from pain. But he clenched his teeth, and a cabbage, if not a rose, began to emerge.

She went on to Bailey Matthews. The ex-cowboy had a small standing loom rigged up, resting on his chest.

"Gosh darn threads! Won't go—" He yanked at the wooden needle. Cherry pitied the helpless fellow, but she knew better than to proffer too much help or sympathy.

Glancing up from his work, Matty shouted at her, "Never mind! It'll look real nice when it's finished!"

Hy and Jim, alongside, were managing nicely between them. They had paints and cardboard, and were designing several posters announcing next week's amateur show, with GI stars. Neither man could yet exercise his injured leg with Occupational Therapy but at least this job kept them busy and interested.

"No acrobats in this show," Hy complained. He scratched his baldish head with his paintbrush. "Just wait till I get better. I'll make their eyes bug out with my tricks!" He wheeled away, saying he needed more supplies.

Jim looked up at Cherry with a smile. "Do you like this color combination?" he asked. "I always did like to mess around with paints."

Jim's poster showed a good deal of taste. Cherry said so, and asked:

"What kind of work do you do, Jim?"

"Used to do," he corrected her. "I was a woodworker and lumber machinist. Worked a machine with a foot treadle. Guess that's out now." He changed the subject and went on to talk about the great forests of Oregon, his state, and the lumber industry there.

Suddenly he was talking about home. It was the first time this reserved young man had confided much to anyone here in the rehabilitation hospital. "It's just a frame house in a little bit of a town. But there are forests and a cold, fast-running river all around my town. The house—well, it's the house my parents always lived in. It's the house I was born in, and my father died in. I'd like to go back to that house and park my feet on the old familiar sofa. My foot, I guess I mean," he said, and managed a chuckle. "I had my own workshop there, and a tool shed. No matter what window in our house you look out of, you see forests, thousands of years old." He stopped and seemed to daydream. "You know, Miss Cherry, trees are alive. And working in wood is—"

"Yes? What?" For Jim's sensitive face had a look on it Cherry had never seen before. It was a look of absorbed and loving interest. This was how Jim must have been before he got hurt—happy, spunky, independent.

"A piece of wood in your hand," he said, his eyes glowing, "is a live thing, crying out to you to make it into something to use. You rub your hands over it to learn its texture, you let your tools follow the natural grain, you sort of dream out a design. You work and work, and pretty soon you have something—something almost beautiful."

Cherry smiled at him. She had respect for an honest, creative, hard-working craftsman. And Jim clearly descended from the tradition of sturdy American craftsmen who hewed the trees of the wilderness into the first American stockades, houses, furniture—those builders and artisans who settled the rough country, armed with little else than imagination and skill and labor.

"It's good and satisfying to work, to make things," said Jim. "I can't say it in words, but I can say it by building a stout fence or a fine chest of drawers or a swing for the neighbors' kids. Miss Cherry, do you think," he asked her anxiously, "and please be honest with me—do you think I'll be dependent the rest of my days?"

"No, no, no! You still have both those skilled hands of yours, haven't you? And it's quite possible you may be able to pump a treadle machine again."

"Hope you're right." Jim sat back against his pillow and looked squarely at her. "I'd rather be dead than be dependent on my mother. You see, my mother is pretty old and frail. She gave up teaching that little country school years ago. But when I enlisted—even though I sent her my pay, which wasn't much—Well, Mother had to go back to teaching. She's perfectly good-humored about her hardships, says she likes to keep busy, as game a little old lady as you ever saw. The kids love her. I sent her a hundred dollars for a vacation but she bought me a War Bond instead. She's all alone out there, too. I want to get back and support her and let her take it easy."

"You will, Jim," Cherry promised. "Honestly, you will be self-supporting again."

Jim sighed in relief. His smile had real sweetness.

"And I was thinking of myself as a cripple! Shucks, I have my health, I have my two hands. Why, sure, I'm all right!" He said it defiantly, as if daring anyone to deny it. He grinned at Cherry. "Heard our joke? We didn't know they took one-legged men like me in the Army." He chuckled quietly.

Cherry drew a long breath. It was the soldiers' typical grim joke. But the very fact that Jim could joke, that Jim could assert "I'm all right," proved he was struggling toward a sound outlook. He still had a long way to go to recovery. Cherry hoped nothing would crack his courage on the way.

Since Cherry was still a floater, odds and ends of assignments came her way. She was pleased when an order came through, later in the week, to escort the patients who had earned "birdies" to an evening party at the Demarest home. Cherry was curious to see for herself the evening parties the other fellows enthusiastically described as going on there.

"You don't *have* to go to the Demarests'," Cherry said to the men as they got ready, about seven o'clock. "You are free to go anywhere in the village you like."

"Oh, so you want to get rid of us!" George teased, as Hy Leader tied his khaki tie for him. "Sorry. We aren't missing out on one of those Demarest parties."

"I wish I could go," muttered redheaded Matty from his cast. Cherry wished so, too. "I'm all dressed in this coffin. Just give me my hat."

Jim was hopping around the aisle on crutches. "Soon as I get the hang of these, I'll be going along too."

"Say, fellows." Matty banged the bed to get attention. "Bring me back a Coke!"

Pernatelli came over to Bailey Matthews with a grin on his face. "You know what happens to guys in body casts?"

"What?"

"They're limited to three Cokes, so they won't swell up and crack the cast," said Ralph delightedly.

Even the Orphan looked happy at the prospect of being invited out. Cherry set out with six soldiers, bandaged, stumbling, on crutches, but in high spirits. In back of them, along the twilight paths, came other nurses with more wounded soldiers. They met and hailed guys going to the Red Cross recreation hall or the Service Club for enlisted men, the bowling alley, PX, or the hospital movies. The patients had the freedom of the hospital grounds, and Cherry was still not used to the sight of men in maroon bathrobes, trench caps, and heavy GI shoes wandering around outdoors. It was a wonder they did not catch colds, but Sal had assured her they never did.

At the guarded hospital gate, the Military Police checked out Cherry and her charges. The men were excited but they seemed strained. It was their first venture into the world outside the hospital—their first test of whether people would look upon them as cripples, or treat them as the normal men they really were. In their anxiety, in their hurt pride and shaken self-confidence, Cherry realized, some of them wore chips on their shoulders.

"Calm down, fellows," she said. "Take it easy, you'll last longer."

"We're not jittery," Ralph almost snapped at her.

"Not jittery, you understand," the ex-acrobat said. "Just a little irritable maybe."

They rode buses, then walked two blocks into the Demarest grounds, all feeling rather tense.

Mrs. Demarest put the men at ease. She herself opened the door and led them through the circular hall into the beautiful sitting room.

"I'm awfully glad you came over," Mrs. Demarest said to the soldiers. Cherry saw a fleeting sadness in her face, but their hostess smiled at them and asked each man his name.

"Sit down, won't you? We're just getting a mock horse race organized, if you want to back one of these little wooden nags. Cards, over there in the corner. Music, if I can get the accordion away from my husband!"

The men were too shy to do anything but sit stiffly. A maid came in with a big tray of cakes and fancy sandwiches. That helped, even though everyone had just tucked away enormous suppers. Mrs. Demarest turned on the phonograph, and Ralph and the Orphan got up to dance with girls invited from the neighborhood. Mr. Demarest came over dangling the accordion.

"Hello! I'm Bill Demarest. Mighty nice to have you fellows here. Hello, Miss Cherry. Can any of you play this thing?"

"I can," Hy Leader said and reached for the accordion eagerly.

"There's a guitar, too." Their host went to the archway of an adjoining room. "And a piano in here. Who wants to play, and sing? Say, we have a real musician here tonight—Arthur—"

Several of the men rose and hobbled into the music room. They competed loudly with the phonograph and the dancers. Out in the circular hallway, men in wheel chairs placed excited bets—for scoring only—on the wooden toy horses. Mr. Demarest wandered around introducing people, and seeing that no one was left out of the fun. He seemed to be enjoying himself at his own party. He, too, Cherry noticed, wore a half-hidden air of sadness.

Mrs. Demarest was talking with quiet George Blumenthal. Cherry listened. She noticed that the hostess neither asked painful questions nor pretended to ignore the fact that George was a returned soldier with an empty sleeve. She admired her tact when Mrs. Demarest said:

"Oh, you have the Purple Heart. May I see it?" She leaned over and admired it on George's khaki blouse. "I hope you have a son who'll want to 'borrow' that."

"I have a daughter," the teacher said proudly.

"I have a son," Mrs. Demarest said. A shadow crossed her face. "Toby is upstairs asleep—or at least I hope he's asleep!"

She turned to Cherry and drew her into the conversation. She kept that conversation lively and light.

The party took a decided turn for the better when Mr. Demarest gathered everyone together and announced:

"We're going to have a treasure hunt! There's treasure to be found somewhere in this house or garden. But first you'll have to discover the dozens of hidden directions about where to find it. They're hidden all over, but I'll give you a hint—try looking behind sofa cushions and under rugs."

All the soldiers were about to dash off when Mr. Demarest called out, "Work in teams! The fellows you came with, and your nurses, make up your team. All right, go to it! And there are some booby prizes hidden, too!"

Cherry had to restrain her six patients from scampering off in all directions at once. They agreed to keep together, at least for the start. Ralph was already burrowing like a mole in the sofa cushions. Other teams were rapidly turning the Demarests' house upside down, but

Cherry saw that valuable knickknacks and breakables were put away for this evening, so they could go ahead and hunt freely.

"I've got it!" Ralph shouted, and came over to their team, waving a slip of paper. "Here, I'll read it! 'Go to the kitchen and look in the oven.'"

Off they went to the kitchen, Hy rolling his wheel chair, the Orphan limping on his cane. In the oven they found, to their disappointment, only a lone muffin.

"Break it open," Cherry suggested. "See, it's half sliced already." She handed it to the Orphan.

The Orphan broke open the muffin and found a note. "If roses are red and violets are blue, follow the path where this clue leads you."

"The garden!" they chorused, and started out the back door.

"There's a rose garden," Cherry told them, "but I forget just where it is."

They passed another group shinnying up an oak tree, and came to the rose garden. But another team had got there before them. Fisticuffs nearly broke out among the men. Cherry and the other nurse insisted:

"There's more than one clue here, you'll see! There's plenty for all the teams!"

Sure enough, the other team found a note tied to a rosebush, and Hy Leader saw a bit of paper fluttering on the leg of a wrought-iron chair.

"'Try the garage,'" he read.

But the garage was a big one, and where would a note be hidden among all these tools and gadgets? Finally Cherry's bright eyes spied a big red paper package propped invitingly on the window sill.

"That's for us!" and they pounced on it and tore off the red wrappings. Inside were boxes of crackerjack—which could not be counted as treasure—but no clues.

Ralph grumbled. "I'm not going to settle for a booby prize. There must be a clue here somewhere." He whistled. "There're prizes in crackerjack! Let's open 'em and see."

They all opened the boxes, crammed their mouths full of crackerjack, and discovered prizes of tin whistles, wooden beads, a toy watch—and another folded slip of paper, in Cherry's package.

From the garage to the piano bench, from piano bench to the side porch, the notes led them. On the side porch, by the light of the moon, they read:

"*Look under the yellow sofa, my friends—*
That is where your treasure hunt ends."

They raced back to the living room and the yellow sofa. George got down on his knees and pulled out a ten-pound box of chocolates.

"We win! We win!" Cherry and her teammates shouted.

"No, *we* win!" the other teams were shouting. Sooner or later, everybody had won. Laden with assorted treasures, the soldiers and their nurses thanked the Demarests and said good night.

Cherry shepherded her group home. They walked slowly out of the Demarest grounds, in the cool night air, laughing and in high spirits. In the village, they headed for the hospital bus stop. On the way a brightly lighted ice-cream parlor attracted Ralph's attention.

"Coke for Matty," he remembered, "and a jumbo double-sweet chocolate frosted for Mrs. Pernatelli's boy."

He went into the ice-cream parlor like a shot, and held the door for the others.

The shabby confectionery was jammed with soldiers from the hospital, and with civilians too. Apparently it was the town meeting place. Cherry did not like the atmosphere in here. It was cheap, ordinary, gossipy. After the fun they had had at the Demarests', this was a distinct letdown.

Cherry was about to suggest not staying, when a man sprang forward and pulled out a chair for George.

"Let me help you, soldier."

"Thank you," said George doubtfully. He looked shamed. He rearranged the chair with his one hand to show that he was not helpless, and only then did he sit down. There was not much for them all to do then, except sit down with George. The teacher and Hy said something to each other under their breaths which Cherry could not hear.

Cherry did not enjoy her sundae very much. She was watching her six men—or rather, she was watching the civilians around them. Most of them were paying no attention but—She wished some of them would not stare, nor look so pitying. She wanted to cry out, "Yes, George lost his right arm! Yes, the Orphan is limping! What of it? They don't want your pity! You're hurting them!" But she merely sat there, miserably unable to think up any conversation to help her six soldiers through their ordeal.

Several young women were chattering away at the next table. Among them Cherry recognized Margaret Heller and typists from the hospital office. Their voices rose so shrilly that Cherry and her patients gave up their desultory efforts to talk, and listened. The office girls were discussing the Demarest child.

"It's incurable."

"Oh, it is not! They could cure it if they could get that new medicine—you know—what's-its-name—"

"But they can't, and the Demarest boy is dying."

Cherry and her charges exchanged glances. There was tragedy upstairs in the Demarest house while they danced and played games downstairs.

"I bet we have that medicine at the hospital. I heard a rumor that—"

"That's supposed to be a secret!"

"Dr. Orchard said—"

"Girls! You're talking too much. And too loudly." This was Margaret Heller. The other girls, subdued, dropped their voices and changed the subject. Cherry glanced at them impatiently. Margaret Heller was right to reprimand the girls for being so careless in their talk. Cherry did respect her for that, at least. Miss Heller seemed to be a responsible person.

Hy Leader reached over and picked up a newspaper left on an adjoining chair. He handed it silently to Cherry. She and the patients leaned around the table together and read:

HOPE FADES FOR BOY
WITH RARE DISEASE

*Form of Extreme Malnutrition
Slowly Wasting Child Away*

> Trumble, Ill., Apr. 12—The hope of Mr. and Mrs. William Demarest of finding a cure for their four-year-old son, Toby, stricken with a rare disease, ebbed today after a medical consultation. Because his system cannot absorb his food, the boy is literally starving to death . . .

"Horrible," Cherry murmured.

George pushed his milk shake away from him.

Ralph stood up. "Let's blow. I'll get the Cokes for Matty and Jim. Let's get out of this dump." He insisted on paying for their refreshments and hurried them out. Cherry knew just how Ralph felt. They returned to the hospital ward considerably less cheerful than when they had started out.

That ice-cream parlor came to have unpleasant associations for Cherry. Particularly after what happened to Jim there, a little later on.

Jim had mastered the crutches. He could now swing along the corridors at a surprisingly rapid pace. Cherry, with the doctor's permission, took him for several walks around the hospital grounds, too. Jim could now navigate by himself—his only difficulty with the crutches was that the other guys hid them. He was eager to go to the village all by himself. Finally he had wangled the doctor's approval and a pass.

Cherry was out in the corridor for a moment, this afternoon, with Sal. She had talked with Sal about this patient of hers whose morale was slower to mend than the other men's.

"And now," said Cherry, "he's off to the village for the afternoon. It certainly means a lot to him—sort of his personal declaration of independence."

"Hmm," said Sal. "I've seen the men meet this—well, this crisis so often. The guys are in wonderful spirits so long as they're together in the hospital. Cheer each other up, share their losses together. But give the public a chance to work on them and—crash!"

"I know," Cherry said soberly. "My fingers are crossed. I just wish Jim weren't so oversensitive."

"See what you can say to arm him in advance." Sal advised.

Cherry tried to warn Jim not to take any little slip-ups too seriously. But Jim was so elated, sprucing up in his khaki jacket, that he only said:

"How can you be so gloomy on a day like this? Why, I'm all right. What do I care what anyone says? I'll be fine, of course I will. Is my cap on straight? Any shopping you want me to do for you?"

When Jim returned two hours later, he no longer was the smiling fellow who had started out. His face was drawn and white. Even the tapping of his crutches on the corridor floor sounded slow, dragging. Cherry ran out to meet him. She drew him onto a couch in the hall, away from the other fellows' questions.

"Here, Miss Cherry." He handed her a little bunch of violets.

"Why, thank you! They're lovely. Oh, Jim—"

He set his crutches aside and flicked a hand at his empty trouser leg. His eyes were burning.

"I'm your nurse, you can tell me."

"All right. I've got to talk or I'll—I'll explode or bawl or yell at somebody."

When Jim got on the bus, a man tried to help him up the step. Jim took a seat by himself. But the man sat down next to him and asked, "How'd you get it, bud?"

"I told him it was none of his business," Jim said angrily. "But then I was sucker enough to explain it was in a tank. Awful hard not to answer. I wish they wouldn't ask."

He had a stroll around the village. He felt a few eyes staring at him but managed to calm down. Then, standing at a street corner waiting to cross, two elderly women came up behind him. They whispered, what a shame, and wasn't it too bad it was hopeless, and such a young man to go through life like that. Of course Jim heard them.

"Made me feel like an outcast. And then I went into that miserable candy store. Never again! There were some high school kids fooling around at the soda fountain. The moment I came in, they all stopped talking. You could have cut the silence with a knife. They—they *looked* at me. The *way* they looked! You'd think I was a freak."

Cherry said fiercely, "They're fools, people like that! They aren't worth taking seriously."

"Oh, that's not all! I ordered a soda and started to unbutton my jacket and a woman rushes over to unbutton it for me. For heaven's sake, couldn't she see I have two hands—even if I only have one leg!"

Cherry muttered that the women probably had only meant to be sympathetic and kind.

"Well, I don't want their pity! Yes, Miss Cherry, it *is* pity!" His vehemence suddenly dropped into melancholy. "Oh, I guess they're right. A one-legged man, unable to do his old work, is an object of pity." Jim studied his hands. He said very low, "And I almost believed I'd be all right again. I was kidding myself. Just kidding myself all the time."

"Jim! Look at the other guys." Cherry argued with him, fought with him, to bolster his crushed confidence.

She pointed out how jittery Ralph was—even aggressive, sturdy Ralph—about going home to Chicago this week end. She reminded him that Hy, who could laugh over anything, was making a trip to St. Joe this Saturday and Sunday only by forcing himself to go.

"Yes, but," Jim countered, "they have their families. Families at least try to be understanding. Look at George Blumenthal's wife—writing him she married a man, not a hand! That's what makes a fellow feel good."

Cherry put her hand on Jim's forehead. He was running a temperature as a result of this afternoon's misadventure. She thought a moment. Jim had no one except his mother far off in Oregon. All the other boys here had their homes or at least some relative within traveling distance of Graham Hospital. The Army tried to assign men to the appropriate Army hospital nearest their homes. But in Jim's case, there was no orthopedic hospital near his home. Even the Texas boy had a sister coming down tomorrow from Chicago to see him. Even the Orphan, Cherry thought, had friends to visit over the week end in Evanston.

"Listen, Jim," Cherry said. "I'm taking you home with me. Pin these violets on my collar, will you?"

CHAPTER VIII

Week End

JIM WAS TO HAVE HAD CHARLIE'S ROOM, FOR OVER Saturday night. But the stairs were a long winding flight, too much for Jim to manage yet on crutches. The downstairs bedroom, seldom used, was hastily made ready. Mr. Ames showed Jim his room.

Mrs. Ames took Cherry aside in the living room and whispered:

"What does Jim like to do?"

Cherry remembered the woodworking. "He likes to make and fix things. Any chores around the house, lady?"

"And what does Jim like to eat?"

"Anything—and lots of it."

Mrs. Ames looked relieved. "Then my only problem is Velva. Velva!" she called. "Velva has been serving us our meals as if we were all going to a fire," Mrs. Ames explained to Cherry. "To call us to dinner, she simply yells. I must ask her not to be so strenuous, with a convalescent around."

Velva hulked in the dining-room doorway, tied into an apron. She seemed even bigger and brawnier than Cherry remembered her—quite capable of tossing the dining-room table out the window if they did not like the way she served. Cherry said hello, and Mrs. Ames explained that a little less nerve-racking manner would be appreciated.

"For instance," Mrs. Ames suggested gently, "when dinner is ready, just come to the door and say, 'Dinner is served.'"

Velva snorted. "That's too fancy for me. I ain't no sissy Easterner."

"Very well, then say 'Dinner is ready.'"

"If you see me comin', you *know* dinner is ready!"

Mrs. Ames pleaded. "Couldn't you just say 'Dinner'?"

Velva looked grumpy. "What's the matter with me shoutin' 'Chow!'" She yelled "Chow!" so loudly that Cherry held on to the arm of her chair. Mr. Ames and Jim coming into the living room looked startled.

"Velva, this is Sergeant Jim Travers. He'll be here tonight and Sunday."

Jim smiled and Velva clucked at him, "Just exactly like my own kid brother only he's dark and you're medium, and he's short and you're tall, and he's a corporal and—"

"—and the sergeant is hungry," Cherry interrupted, laughing.

Velva looked sternly at Cherry and smiled at Jim. "Down to Turkey Run, we know all about boys being hungry." She withdrew.

"Turkey Run?" Jim said, easing himself into a chair. "Is that a real name?" He was much more at home here than Cherry had dared hope for. She looked gratefully at her father.

"Certainly it's a real name, and a real place," said Mr. Ames. "We get all our poultry from there. Speaking of funny names, we have here in town a Justice Stifler—a Dr. Slaughter—a dentist named Grind—"

"—the Realistic Beauty Shoppe," Mrs. Ames supplied.

"And that lunch counter," Cherry put in, "with the sign, 'Eat here before we both starve!'"

Jim grinned. "In my town, there's a dog and cat hospital with a butcher shop right next door."

Cherry groaned and sang under her breath, "Put another dog in the sau-sage ma-chine . . ."

"Cherry! Jim!" Mrs. Ames had turned slightly green. "Considering that we have hot dogs in the kitchen— Good ones, too, that I bought at the Grab It."

"At the *what*, ma'am?" Jim asked incredulously.

"A grocery named Grab It Here," Mrs. Ames said. "And underneath it says 'Where Ma Saves Pa's Dough.' We'll drive you past it."

Suddenly Velva's voice boomed, way out in the kitchen. They all were startled. Mrs. Ames started to rush out there, when Velva marched to the doorway.

"Chow! Come 'n' git it!" she shouted, and beamed at them.

Jim was sweating at the uproar.

"Thunderation, I forgot," she said. "You wanted me to do it quiet and nice."

"Yes," said Mrs. Ames weakly. "If you will. But wait!—wait a minute—"

But Velva had gone out and now re-entered. She opened her mouth and stole a glance at Mrs. Ames.

"It's on the table!" she sang out. "Grab yourself a plate, folks!"

They went in to dinner, advising Mrs. Ames that she was being very competently spoofed.

After dinner, they drove through Hilton and out past the farms for a few miles. The evening fields were sweet and green. But Mr. Ames said there were "too many Saturday night drivers" reckless on the road. They settled instead for a movie. Jim won, of all things, a soup tureen, which he presented to Mrs. Ames. Then a round of chocolate sodas, brought out to the car so Jim would not have to get out, wound up their evening.

They made their good nights in the hall. Cherry said:

"Pretty tame, I'm afraid, Jim."

"Nothing of the sort, Miss Cherry! It's what I've been missing—being home."

"Well, good night— Dad turned the lamps on in your room—"

"Sleep late!" Mrs. Ames called. "Breakfast whenever you get up!"

"Yes," said Jim happily. "'Night." He hobbled off with a detective novel in his hand and contentment on his face.

No one slept late next morning, for at seven-thirty the phone rang. It rang long and loud before Cherry could stumble down the stairs and seize the raucous thing. It was Midge.

"I called to ask you and your guest over to dinner," Midge's voice squeaked over the wire. "Answer yes or no right away. I have to have plenty of time to get ready."

Cherry's answer was what she thought of people who woke up sleeping households early on Sunday morning. "Besides, I have to ask the others. I'll call you back."

"I'll cook you a dinner such as you never ate before," came out of the receiver. "With music and flowers, too."

Cherry shuddered. "The idea is to cure this boy, not kill him off," she stated, and hung up. She recalled what uproar Midge could wreak with mere flowers and music. She also remembered Dr. Joe's description of Midge's cooking—"a catastrophe. You have to have a cast-iron stomach."

The phone promptly rang again.

"If you decide to come," Midge squeaked, "you'd better come over and help me."

"Go away! Stop phoning! You awful child!"

Cherry was halfway up the stairs, yawning, when the phone rang a third time.

"I'm sorry," said Midge, and hung up without delay.

There was no sound from the others. Cherry went back to bed, asleep again before her head touched the pillow.

When she awoke, the sun was pouring into her room as if it were ten o'clock. It was, in fact, ten o'clock. She jumped out of bed.

"Poor Midge, waiting all this time for a reply!" Cherry thought guiltily. She showered and dressed in haste, and fled downstairs. Only her mother was still at the breakfast table, pretty and fresh in a blue dress.

"Good morning, dear," Mrs. Ames said. "The masculine contingent is out in the garage. Midge has been over here asking us to dinner."

"The only entertainment Midge can ever think of is food," Cherry observed. "How does she fill in the time between meals?"

"She sustains herself with snacks." Mrs. Ames's brown eyes danced. "Do you think Midge would survive the disappointment if we turned her down?"

"Do you think we'd survive her cooking?" Cherry thoughtfully sipped some coffee. "I'll go take a vote."

She left her mother with the voluminous Sunday paper and went out through the back porch, to the back yard and the garage.

Mr. Ames and Jim were in the garage tinkering around with the car. They were both smudged with grease and deep in a discussion. Cherry came and sat down on the running board. She liked the rich smell of gasoline, the pungent smell of the rubber tires.

"Hello," she said again, having been ignored the first time. "Jim, how do you like our Nellie? The car, I mean. We always name our cars."

Mr. Ames patted the fender. "This one's named Nellie because she's slow, dumpy, and comfortable."

Jim said, "Mine's called Joe. Not elegant but he gets me there. My first little jalopy, when I was in high school, I named Leopold. Because he sat up so high and comical on his little wheels, and looked so old-fogey."

"My brother's ambition," Cherry said, "is to own a car worthy of the name of The Duke. Big, black, dignified, and fast."

Jim confided, "I've named my crutches. Never told you in the hospital. They're Ike and Mike. Mike is a little slower than Ike, because I'm not as deft with my left hand as with my right one."

"Of course, Ike and Mike won't be with you long," she reminded Jim. "You are going to abandon them without a pang, for a nice new leg."

"Of course I am," Jim said confidently.

Mr. Ames looked suddenly sober but kept on poking in the engine. Cherry brought up the question of

Midge's invitation. She supplied, for Jim, a description of the Fortune household and added, "At your own risk."

Jim hemmed and hawed politely, and finally admitted he would like to go. "But first," he said very eagerly, "your mother told me there's a door and a bureau drawer that stick. And your father gave me a fine piece of bird's-eye maple. Do you suppose I could—"

"In that tone of voice, you certainly could." Cherry laughed. "Plenty of time to get over to the Fortunes'. And I am *not* going to go over and worm Midge out of her Midge-made messes. I gave her a whole Sunday recently, and that's enough. She'll have to battle the burners and pitch pots and pans on her own."

So Jim happily hammered and whittled, while Cherry grubbed for early violets along the side fence. Then they went for a little walk up and down Cherry's tree-shaded block. Some of the neighbors were already sitting out on their front porches, although in warm coats. They called hello to Cherry and Jim, and Mrs. Pritchard came down her steps to give them a crock of cookies she had made. Jim blossomed at being accepted so readily.

Lunch was late and peaceful because Velva was not there. Cherry washed dishes and Jim, sitting on the kitchen ladder, dried them. Cherry noticed again the sweetness in his face. Sunday afternoon dragged along. They were leisurely getting ready to drive over to the Fortunes', about five o'clock, when the doorbell rang.

"Please let me in," said Dr. Joe rather desperately. "My own house isn't fit to live in."

He wandered into the living room, shaking his gray head, and sat down with his overcoat still on.

"What's happened?" the Ameses asked, while Jim stayed modestly in the background.

Dr. Joe thought, then replied methodically, "First, the stove caught on fire. Second, Midge perfumed the house with onions. I abhor onions. Third, she played that fool record all day. I believe my love of music has come to an end. Fourth, I had no lunch. Fifth, Midge used my best crucible to mash Roquefort cheese in. And sixth, the roast we were to have had for dinner burned to a crisp and Midge wept copiously. Seventh— Seventh— Oh, yes. Seventh, I believe I had no breakfast either, if I recollect."

They clustered around the elderly man, bringing him milk and bread and butter, and helping him off with his overcoat. Dr. Fortune with a woebegone face drinking milk in an outfit of khaki trousers, gray flannel jacket, sweater for a shirt, and sneakers, was an astonishing sight.

Cherry said, with as much formality as possible under the circumstances, "Dr. Fortune, this is Sergeant Jim Travers. Jim, Dr. Fortune is Lieutenant Colonel Fortune of the Army Medical Corps, but he's home on sick leave."

Jim stood very straight on his crutches and tried to salute.

Dr. Joe waved a piece of bread and butter at Jim. "Never mind the formalities, my boy. Just look at me." He glanced down at his absent-minded choice of clothes. "It's this difficult matter of becoming a civilian again," he confided to Jim with a chuckle. "Just wait until you get out of khaki and have to decide daily what to put on."

"Yes, sir. But what became of your daughter?" Jim asked curiously.

That was answered promptly. The doorbell rang. Midge practically fell into the hallway, her eyes red from weeping. She gave out a distinct aroma of burned onions. Cherry unobtrusively opened a window. Everyone tried hard to keep a straight face.

Mr. Ames said in a hearty voice, "Midge, we were just trying to decide where to go for dinner—the Lincoln Hotel or Dick's for steaks. What do you say?"

Midge looked suspiciously from one face to another. She looked a long time at Jim's open countenance. Then in a very small voice indeed she said:

"Dick's would be nice, thank you. In fact—Dick's would be *wonderful!*"

Jim never did dine at the Fortunes' on Midge's cuisine. But late that evening, as the Ameses let him and Cherry out of the car at the hospital gate, he said:

"Thank you. I'm really obliged to you. Now the home feel has soaked in!"

CHAPTER IX

Clues

THE HOSPITAL WAS ELECTRIFIED. THE STAFF PEOPLE were shocked and buzzing with excitement. There had been a robbery in the medical storeroom!

Cherry sought out Sal Steen at six-thirty breakfast in Officers' Mess. "Tell me all you know," she demanded sleepily. For Sal, an old-timer here, always was well informed. Even about a theft that occurred in the middle of last night.

Sal's colorless face was almost animated, for once, over this excitement.

"It's that new and special amino acid medicine. You know—that rare and valuable drug. Someone took it out of its locked compartment in the medical storeroom."

Cherry asked, "The place you called Nephalogy and sent me for a joke?"

"Yes. Only it isn't such a joke, as it turns out. We need that medicine to speed up our patients' recovery. A lot of them need it—only there isn't nearly enough. And now some has been stolen into the bargain."

Cherry shook her dark curls. "Aren't there any clues? Any theories?"

"Plenty of theories but no clues. That medicine is kept locked up in the storeroom and guarded like the crown jewels. The Army pharmacist is there all day and at night there's a watchman."

"Who has keys?" Cherry asked carefully. "Or who could get hold of keys?"

"The pharmacist has the keys, naturally, and so has the Principal Chief Nurse. Also a few head doctors and a few head nurses who use special medicines have duplicate keys. And the whereabouts of each key is carefully accounted for at all hours to the main office."

"But it must have been done by someone who somehow has access to a key," Cherry concluded. "Also, obviously, it must have been done by someone here in the hospital, not an outsider."

"Obviously, huh?" Sal sniffed. "It's not so simple as that. There's something else funny. The thief, whoever it was, opened the outside door to the storeroom with a key. He got hold of that key somehow. But he didn't use a key to open the particular compartment where this medicine is kept. I suppose that key's so doubly precious he couldn't get hold of that one. The lock to the compartment was *picked*."

Cherry stared wide-eyed at Sal, who was obviously enjoying her role as the dispenser of such sensational news.

"And if you want extra complications," Sal continued, "try thinking about the thief's motive. Why would anyone want to steal that stuff anyway? Amino acid medicines are still so new that very few people, even doctors, know exactly or fully how to use them. No doctor or nurse or scientist in his right mind—"

"Or with any sense of ethics," Cherry quickly interrupted. "He'd lose his standing. And no nonmedical person would have any use for it. Would he? Unless someone stole it to sell it for money. He could, couldn't he?"

Sal thought a moment, then shrugged her shoulders. "I can't figure it out."

"Well, find the thief's motive and you've solved half the mystery," Cherry said as she rose to go to her ward.

"Smart girl, Cherry! Are *you* going to solve the mystery?" Sal inquired dryly.

"I?" Cherry laughed. "Oh, certainly. In five minutes."

The problem tantalized her, as she hurried along the covered walk to Orthopedic Building. It was a sunny cheerful morning, with the trees and lawns all bright green, and the squirrels and birds chattering at each other. Streams of uniformed medical people in the wooden walk briskly went to morning duties. Cherry caught snatches of their conversation. They were talking about the theft.

"Must have been an inside job—must have!"

"Were any of the keys missing?"

"Anyone in our main office ought to be able to guess its value and where it's kept—"

"No doctor would dare do such a thing!"

At the open door of Orthopedic Ward, Cherry prompted herself. "Now forget about the mystery," and she put it away in another compartment of her mind. "For the time being," she qualified, and went in.

The patients were having breakfast, corpsmen were cleaning and straightening the ward. Cherry flew about making herself useful at small tasks. There was a newcomer helping on the ward this morning—a nurse in the first white starched uniform Cherry had seen here.

The nurse in white kept very much to herself. Cherry tried to be friendly and started to talk with her, over a stack of bandages. Since the mystery, at the moment, was the general topic of conversation, it was only natural that Cherry should comment on it.

To her surprise, the nurse snapped crossly:

"I'm doing my work and minding my own business. Why don't you do the same? There's plenty to be done right here, without all you people trying to play detective."

Cherry recoiled from the vehemence in the woman's words and tone. "Well—" Cherry started to answer.

"Lieutenant Ames," the young chief nurse cut in crisply from her desk, "it's time to get your patients ready for the Reconditioning Officer."

Cherry was grateful to the chief nurse for this reminder. She was only too happy for the opportunity to move away from this very unpleasant woman—in fact, the quicker the better!

She went quickly from bed to bed, getting the patients ready for the Reconditioning Officer and their exercises. It was heartening to see how many of them now could get out of bed and stand to exercise. Even redheaded Matty was in a sitting-up cast now, and Jim was in such good spirits he looked like a different fellow.

As Cherry worked, she was bothered by the feeling that the nurse's violent reaction to the robbery was very strange. Why? Cherry wondered. Curious to find out more about the woman, she stole a moment in the laboratory to ask Edith Randall about the nurse in the white uniform.

"She's a civilian nurse," the pretty Edith explained. "Name's Miss Lacey. She was rejected by the Army Nurse Corps and that's why she's not in khaki or seersucker uniform. She works here at Graham on a fairly permanent basis. And I think she lives in the village."

"Oh, these civilian nurses can't live in Army Nurses' Quarters?" Cherry asked.

"She could live in Nurses' Quarters if she wished to. Evidently she prefers to live in the village. Maybe her family's there." Edith giggled. "Or maybe she's in love with a local yokel."

Cherry was thoughtful as she went back to her duties. Nothing that Edith had told her explained why Miss Lacey had been so violent on the subject of the mystery. A sudden thought struck Cherry. "Guilty people often gave themselves away when someone innocently touched on the subject of their crime." Could it be possible that Miss Lacey knew something about the theft?

Cherry's vivid imagination immediately saw her armed to the teeth with picklocks and stolen keys.

This mental picture of the plump, grouchy Miss Lacey pulled Cherry up short. "Good heavens! You can't go around pinning crimes on people who are short-tempered," she argued with herself. "Her explosiveness is probably not the result of crimes in the night—more likely her feet hurt her."

And with that conclusion, Cherry dismissed the nurse in white from her mind.

The morning streaked along. Before Cherry realized it, numbers of men were deserting the ward for the crafts shops. Jim, too, was going to Occupational Therapy room for the first time this morning. Cherry was to take him over there, and to deliver the doctor's therapy prescription, for the right work to improve

Jim's particular physical condition. The ward was almost empty as they left. The hospital's census was low, no new wounded had arrived recently. Those who did remain in bed were studying courses from their own high schools and colleges, aiming for graduation. Out in the corridor, a patient with burned hands was playing the piano.

"He plays a little more each day," Jim told her. "Things like that make you feel good inside."

"Don't they, though," said Cherry, and wondered who could be mean enough to steal medicine from soldiers as brave as these.

Cherry was interested in going to the Occupational Therapy room. She had seen this room before, but briefly. This morning, while the O.T. officer got Jim settled, she lingered.

Occupational Therapy was in two big sunny halls. It was quiet in here, neither melancholy nor cheerful. Men worked at scattered tables, not talking, and trained Red Cross Gray Ladies kept calm watch. Cherry saw a patient she knew from Orthopedic: with his stiff, too pale fingers, he tried over and over, painfully, patiently, trembling a little, to tighten a screw in a chair leg. The men's faces with the lowered eyes were a little tense too. Their smiles at Cherry were polite, remote. Some of them, Cherry guessed, were calming down here after shattering emotional experiences. One man with a foreign face and a thoroughly American grin was weaving at a loom. When Cherry admired his blue-and-white rug, he said:

"Yes, thank you, it's coming out nicely. Do you think I should fringe the edges or leave them plain?" Abruptly his face tightened, his voice changed. "This is just a hobby with me. I'm not living. I'm just marking time."

None of the men wanted to talk. Cherry knew their unwritten law: they would not talk about the horrible things seen in combat. Stubbornly, silently, they worked at the leather, woolens, wood—working their way back to health.

Jim was ready now. The O.T. instructor had stood him before a press, pumping a knee-height treadle, to regain lost circulation in his stump. The press punched holes in belts.

"Well," said Jim philosophically to Cherry, "if I have to do this to get well, I have to do it. Maybe I can work that machine over there next." He nodded toward a machine which heaped curly wood shavings on the floor. The wood smelled fresh and good.

"I'll ask the O.T. officer for you," Cherry promised him. She questioned him whether the treadle was reasonably comfortable for his leg, then spoke with the O.T. officer. Before leaving, Cherry arranged with Jim for him to go on next to the Physical Therapy rooms, where water, air, radio, electricity, massage, would stimulate his deadened leg back to life. Then, later, an artificial leg could be worked by those live muscles. "Keep a stiff upper lip and you'll soon be walking," she encouraged him.

"You bet," Jim said and calmly set to pumping his press.

Cherry left O.T. and headed for the Receiving-and-Evacuation Building on the open paths. In this building soldiers arrived for admission to Graham, and departed on transfer or discharge. More important, this was the building where soldiers came for passes. A short cut of bare earth was worn across the grass, making it clear these men loved—and sought—liberty.

In the barnlike building, Cherry hunted up the brisk young lieutenant in charge. He supplied the information she needed about a patient. Cherry noticed that he looked very amused and asked why. He broke into a chuckle.

"We're disciplining Peters again," he said. "What! You haven't heard about Peters? Why, he's our prize problem boy."

First the lieutenant explained that upon admission the men's clothes were taken away from them and locked in the basement and were released to them only on occasions when they received passes. However, despite this precaution, some of the patients would climb out of bed, manage to get some clothes, and calmly go AWOL. Peters, minus his clothes, had managed to go AWOL eight times.

"No, no!" the young man said hastily, as Cherry's face changed. "Peters did wear something. We never did find out exactly how he got the clothes. Well—"

When Peters had a two-day pass, he stayed five days. The last time he was gone, minus pass or permission, minus cash and clothes, for two weeks. Reducing his rank and pay from sergeant's to private's did not faze him. The lieutenant did not know how he got along outside for so long without money, but he did. Peters had again been currently wandering.

"Where's your problem child now?" Cherry asked laughingly.

"Down in the basement doing his discipline routine," the lieutenant grinned.

"What makes you so sure about that?" Cherry teased.

The young lieutenant's face straightened: "Oh, gosh!" he exclaimed. "I guess I'd better check again. That guy is a whiz at picking locks."

It was Cherry's turn to sober, for suddenly Sal's words echoed in her ears:

"That lock was *picked*."

Cherry's thoughts started racing. Who was this Peters who was so adept at picking locks? And why was he so eager to get away from the hospital? She recalled her remark to Sal: "Find the thief's motive and you've solved half the mystery." Could Peters, whom everyone regarded as a comic, have stolen and sold the amino medicine? Was this why he went AWOL—and how he sustained himself for days, seemingly without funds?

Curious to see the fellow, Cherry asked the lieutenant if she could accompany him while he checked on Peters. The lieutenant agreed, and Cherry followed him downstairs into a spacious basement. He unlocked a door into a sort of cell. There on the cot snored a tousled young man of about eighteen, happy-go-lucky even in sleep. He was clothed in a blanket and tucked in his GI shoes on the floor were some timetables.

"This is Peters," said the young officer softly and shut the door again.

"If Peters is a criminal," Cherry muttered to herself—"then I am Minnie Mouse!" she exclaimed aloud.

The young officer looked puzzled for a moment and then grinned at her. "Huh! Good-looking mice we have nowadays!"

It was a subdued Cherry who went back to Nurses' Quarters. After stopping in the mail room, it was a very bright-eyed and delighted Cherry. For here was a letter from Captain Wade Cooper, AAF pilot, who had flown Cherry's ambulance plane when she was a flight nurse. Why, she had thought Wade was still in England! Cherry grinned as she remembered the good times she and Wade had shared together. She tore open his letter eagerly.

"Dear darling Lieutenant," he had scrawled,

"I am coming home and the first bit of U.S.A. I want to see is you. I'll go home first to Tucson to see parents and suchlike. Then you are to invite me to Hilton for a week end. I hereby accept. It'll be very soon, so dust off your dancing shoes. I won't write any more than this—I'll tell you everything in person. And I mean *everything*. Don't marry anyone till I get there.

"Love, love, love—Wade."

Whee! That was wonderful news! Cherry felt so happy about the prospect of seeing Wade again that she voted herself the evening off at the movies. She would not even ask anyone to go with her this evening. She wanted to gloat in private about a bronzed young flier named Wade Cooper.

It was a fine movie, full of blood-and-thunder mystery, and people so clever that they could have solved the hospital robbery, Cherry thought, while brushing their teeth. If she could just get that suave detective to step off the screen and into the medical storeroom—

Then, to Cherry's amazement, when the newsreel came on, she was looking full into the gigantic screen faces of Ann, Gwen, Bertha, Josie, and Mai Lee! Yes, there were all of her old schoolmates—in Army nurse uniform—in England, helping send the wounded soldiers home. Gwen's red hair did not show up as red, but Gwen was laughing puckishly as usual, and every freckle showed! When Ann's serene gaze met Cherry's gaze, and Ann spoke, Cherry almost talked back to her. It was all she could do not to bounce out of her seat and go running up to them. There came Josie, scared of the camera, and skirting it with a rabbity, sidelong glance. And there stood the little Chinese-American girl Mai Lee—she looked so tired that Cherry's heart went out to her. And Bertha, plump as ever—and didn't that fair hair in the background belong to Marie Swift? Suddenly the newsreel switched and Cherry lost their familiar faces, found herself confronted instead with a homely man making a speech. She got up in a dazed, happy way, and went to the box office.

"When will that newsreel of nurses be shown again?"

"Sorry, that was the last showing tonight. And the program changes tomorrow."

Oh, well. She had had a good, satisfying look at them, anyway. Almost a visit! It left her aglow. Only Vivian Warren was not in the picture, though Cherry knew Vivian was with them in England. The girls and Cherry had been corresponding regularly. But newsreel pictures brought them so very near!

Cherry ambled down the village street to the hospital bus, lost in reverie. Seeing Ann and Gwen and Mai Lee had brought all sorts of memories flooding back: the merry, foolish times when they were student nurses together—the still unbelievable hardships and dangers of their Pacific island field hospital—how lovely Ann had looked that winter's day in England when she married Jack, her beautiful bridal gown fashioned from a bed sheet!

The bus driver had to tell Cherry twice that they were at the hospital gate.

She strolled off down the dusky hospital paths, still daydreaming. If it thrilled her so to see the girls on a movie screen, imagine how she would feel when Wade showed up in person! She wished he would hurry up and get to Hilton. On these thrilling spring evenings, she could do with a spot of romance.

Distant music gradually penetrated her consciousness. It came from the Officers' Club, and it reminded her that that was a fine, cheerful place to go on a spring night. She had managed all too few visits there. Cherry brightened and trotted off at a livelier pace.

Glowing windows and the strains of a trio playing dance music welcomed her. Officer patients and nurses, some together, some alone, were pouring into the handsome little brick loggia. Cherry knew only very few of them. She entered and stood for a moment enjoying the loveliness and gaiety of this room.

It was a big, long, low room, like a lounge. Decorative Chinese murals were painted on the pale-blue brick walls. In one corner, up on a dais, was a huge gray stone fireplace, with banquettes built all around it. Out in the glass-enclosed veranda were little tables and chairs, café fashion. Another small room held a radio and television machine and couches, and there was a brightly painted cardroom. The place was crowded with men and young women in khaki, dancing, chatting, wandering around. Hot jazz poured out of the grand piano.

"Cherry!" someone called. "Over here!"

It was Sal Steen. She was with two young fliers, both on crutches.

"Cherry, I had a hunch you'd come. I saved a seat for you."

Cherry squeezed in with them on a long sofa and was introduced to the young men.

"Sorry we can't dance," they said. "Would you like something to drink?"

"I'd love a Coke."

One of the fellows went off to get it for her. Cherry felt a little guilty about letting a wounded flyer wait on her. But she knew how good it was for them to do things by themselves. He came limping back and presented the Coke to her with a flourish.

"Why, thank you, gallant sir," Cherry giggled. "I'll come over to your ward and nurse you right and left any time."

"I wish you would, I'm in Officers' Ward 2," he said.

Cherry transferred her dark gaze to Sal. Sal's biscuit-colored face was flushed and her pale hair brushed to a sheen: she looked surprisingly pretty.

"Could you guess what we were talking about when you came in?" Sal asked Cherry.

"Love," said Cherry.

"No, we—"

"But that's an idea," said the smitten flyer. Cherry grinned at him and advised him that her coke was very, very good.

"Guess," the second young officer said, leaning forward on the couch so the four of them made a tight little group.

"What you're going to do when you get out of the Army," Cherry guessed. "No?"

"We have a complaint. Here it's spring and we haven't had any spring celebration!" Sal chanted mournfully, "No May Day party, no nothin'—on account of Colonel Winifred Brown."

"I guess the Principal Chief Nurse doesn't believe in spring or parties," the second officer said with a smile.

"What's the matter with having a May Day party right here and now?" Cherry asked.

Sal unwound herself to a standing position. "And I'll be Queen of the May." She struck a comical pose. "Come let us go a-Maying!—whatever that is. Come dance around the Maypole!"

The young nurses and officers around them glanced at Sal with appreciation. They were used to her crazy, zany humor. It infected them too: their eyes sparkled.

Sal stretched out long arms to them, and called out, "Come dance around the Maypole, kiddies. No charge. Meet the Queen of the May. Yippee!"

Two men from another group came over waving a paper napkin. "We crown you Queen of the May!" and they perched a paper napkin crown on Sal's head. To the trio they called, "A little May Day music, please!" The musicians struck up a trilling tune.

Three nurses lugging branches of forsythia out of a vase danced over to Sal, and danced around her. They cried, "For she's the Queen of the May, tra la! Some queen!"

The two men with Cherry stacked two of their crutches together. "It's a Maypole!" They seized the forsythia and stuck it on the crutches. More people surged over, to join in the growing pandemonium. A snake line formed around the Maypole, shouting, laughing, chanting something about, "It's May, hurray!"

And in the middle of it all capered Sal, hanging on to her paper crown, whirling Cherry around her, brandishing someone's cane for a wand.

"Everybody pair off!" Sal shouted. "Follow me!"

Young men and young women exuberantly locked arms, and followed Sal in a crazy game of Follow the Leader. Over the sofa back she went, with two dozen of them scrambling after her—on her hands and knees among the small tables on the veranda with all of them crawling and laughing—dancing like imps around the mock Maypole, with belts for Maypole ribbons—toasting each other in Cokes, striking lampoon attitudes, bedlam egged on by Sal—

Suddenly a whistle blew in the room. Everyone sharply fell silent. Who on earth was blowing a whistle—intruding military discipline *here*? Was there an emergency of some sort?

Hatchet-faced Colonel Brown tooted her whistle again from the doorway.

"It's twelve o'clock!" she snapped. "High time you all were in bed! I'm putting the lights out in two minutes. Out, now. Out!"

The Principal Chief Nurse had no authority to do this to her nurses, and she had absolutely no authority at all over the men officers. But no one was going to brave that bristling little figure. They all scampered out.

"Joy-killer," Sal muttered under her breath. "Wet blanket. Pickle puss."

"I knew it was too good to last," whispered Cherry's swain. "Good night!"

Cherry headed for Nurses' Quarters with Sal, scolding:

"The only mystery around here is how that woman knows every last little thing that's going on—and manages to be in four places at once!"

CHAPTER X

A Turn for the Better

THE NEXT TIME CHERRY WENT TO TELL TOBY DEMAREST a story she found his parents transformed. Their sad, haunted look was erased. Mrs. Demarest almost sparkled. Toby's father stood up straighter, walked and talked with a new zest. The change could mean only one thing.

"Toby's better! Oh, Cherry, he's so much better! It's a near miracle. Come up and see for yourself!"

Cherry ran up the stairs with Mrs. Demarest, tingling, and hoping this wonderful news was really true. She burst in the door, not even waiting for the private duty nurse to admit them.

Toby was sitting up cross-legged in bed, looking around with interest, talking absorbedly to himself. He had visibly gained weight, and there was actually some color in his face.

"Why, Toby! Don't you look fine!" Cherry exclaimed joyfully.

"H'lo. I've got red cheeks like you now," the little fellow boasted.

"Well, three cheers for you! Shake, pardner!"

"Wonderful, isn't it?" Mrs. Demarest beamed. Toby's nurse looked happy too, as she tactfully left the room.

"I'm goin' to get up," Toby said. "An' go for a walk an' a ride an' see a circus."

Cherry pretended to be overwhelmed and had to steady herself on a chair. "Aren't you a smart boy to get well so fast!"

"The smart one," Mrs. Demarest said in a low voice, "is our young Dr. Orchard. You know he's in sole charge of Toby now. All the specialists withdrew from the case."

Cherry was surprised. "They all gave Toby up? Except Dr. Orchard? And this young local doctor—you're leaving it all to him?"

Mrs. Demarest nodded. Cherry made no comment. She was too puzzled to know what to think or say. Except that Toby's improvement was a cause for rejoicing—and so sudden it took her breath away. This Dr. Orchard must be a wonder-worker. How had he accomplished this? What medicines or foods or methods had he used, to get such immediate and spectacular results?

Cherry stood beside Toby's bed. The sharpness of her relief was a revelation to her. She had always recognized that the little boy tugged at her heart—as he would at anybody's. But she put Jim and her other patients and her hospital work definitely first. She had kept Toby separate, in a way, from the rest of her life, and never talked of him at the hospital lest it be depressing. Only now did Cherry realize how much these afternoons with the child, snatched from the main current of her days, had endeared Toby to her. And how deeply, apparently, the little boy had grown to feel for her.

He was tugging at her hand. "Tell me a story 'bout giants!" he demanded.

Cherry sat down by his bed and told him one of the Scandinavian fairy tales, of marvelous creatures greater than men who roamed the mountain forests and fiords. Mrs. Demarest smiled as Toby's blue eyes grew rounder and rounder.

"And next time," Cherry finished, "you shall hear about the tall, bearded, blue-eyed Vikings who came down from those same snowy mountains, out of the northern mists, to sail the seas as no men have ever done before or since."

Toby was breathless. "They was real men? Not made up?"

Cherry nodded. "Real men, who discovered North America, way back when the calendar read ten hundred and something."

"Whew! Tell me now. Right now."

"We-ell—since you're so much better—What do you think, Mrs. Demarest?"

But the door opened just then, and in came—not a Viking out of Toby's imagination—but short, plump, cold Dr. Orchard. He looked at all of them sharply.

"Good afternoon, Mrs. Demarest, Lieutenant Ames, Hello, Toby." There was no extra warmth in his voice for the child.

"Miss Ames has been marveling at your wonderful results with our boy," Mrs. Demarest said graciously.

"Indeed!" Dr. Orchard's voice was frigid. Then abruptly he changed his manner. He twinkled at them and said in a genial voice, "Well, it's a great day when we can bring the boy around."

"It's certainly a great credit to you, Dr. Orchard," Cherry said. "Toby's improved remarkably. May I ask how—"

"Doctor, do you think my son will—" Mrs. Demarest broke in anxiously.

"Now, now, my dear Mrs. Demarest. Please don't expect too much all at once. I've already told you this improvement is only temporary."

"Only temporary?" Cherry exclaimed. Some of her joy fled. She thought anxiously that they should not be saying all these things before the small patient. He could understand.

"Yes, only temporary," Dr. Orchard repeated firmly. "Unless—" He closed his mouth tightly.

"Unless what?" Mrs. Demarest begged. "We'll do everything possible to cooperate with you—you know that!"

Dr. Orchard made no reply. Cherry was puzzled at his silence. And if this improvement was only temporary—then why—?

Cherry asked the young doctor respectfully, "What medicines or drugs have you used, Dr. Orchard, to achieve such fine results?"

"I am not yet ready to say," he evaded. At Cherry's look of surprise, he added, "I'm not sure a nurse would fully understand the explanation anyway."

Cherry accepted this quietly, but she thought it an odd answer. Any good nurse would understand medical technique.

Toby whispered, "Tell me 'bout the Vikings."

Cherry whispered back, "They've gone home for the day."

"Well, tell 'em Toby wants to see the Vikings."

"What's that?" Dr. Orchard said. "Oh, yes, the storytelling. Mr. and Mrs. Demarest told me about it. Very kind of you, Miss Ames. By the way, if you're really interested in my method of cure—" He smiled at Cherry ingratiatingly. "It is not so much a matter of any one thing as a combined technique of medication, diet and treatment."

Cherry thanked him. But she found this answer, too, rather dissatisfying. It was so vague. Still, she supposed Dr. Orchard had valid reasons for not wishing to discuss his techniques just yet. At least he was honest enough to warn the Demarests that Toby's improvement was only temporary, and not lead them to fruitless hopes.

Dr. Orchard bent over the child. Toby looked at Dr. Orchard, not with his usual trusting look, and drew away slightly.

Cherry turned aside. Well, it was only natural that Toby would dread the person who submitted him to all sorts of uncomfortable regimens. Too bad the doctor treating a youngster could not be a more sympathetic personality.

She said good-bye to Toby, who wailed in protest, and hastily left the room with Mrs. Demarest.

Young Mr. Demarest was standing in the circular hallway waiting for them, as they descended the stairs.

"Isn't it wonderful!"

"It *is* wonderful, Mr. Demarest," Cherry agreed.

"We had felt so helpless. Of course this improvement may not last, but still it gives us reason to hope."

"It's so good to see our son looking like himself again," Mrs. Demarest murmured.

Their faces glowing, they pressed Cherry's hands and asked her to come back again soon. "He'll be so much better, right along," they promised. "Oh, he'll be up and walking soon—playing with other children—everything!"

Cherry hoped so. But as she went soberly back to the hospital, she remembered Dr. Orchard's warning. Toby's improvement was only temporary.

CHAPTER XI

Wade Comes to Town

WADE CAME TO HILTON ON A BEAUTIFUL MAY EVENING. He was in a romantic mood. So was Cherry "—or at least, I *want* to feel romantic toward *somebody* in this palpitating spring weather!" she had thought. In the days after she had received Wade's letter saying he was coming, she had made arrangements. Wangled Saturday and Sunday off—which meant Friday evening free, too. Telephoned her mother and father frantically to prepare themselves for still another house guest. Brushed her hair, polished up her face, and splurged with a new bottle of perfume. She even borrowed Midge's technique—with moderation—of filling the rooms with spring flowers.

Here she sat on the porch swing, Friday evening. The moon shone silver. The purple clematis vine screening the porch bloomed and was fragrant. The whole dreaming street swam in moonlight and leaf shadows, as if under water, as if enchanted.

"If only I could wear a soft dress instead of this regulation beige one," Cherry mourned to herself. But she knew her eyes were very dark and bright tonight, her vivid face glowing like a red rose.

She thought of Wade. She had never really been in love with him. Perhaps because there had never been time or occasion in those hectic flying days. But this tender night might change everything. Tonight, with peace and solitude and time to dream, and her heart already stabbed by spring—tonight and these three days could be—"oh, *everything*," she whispered.

The whole thing was dreamlike. Wade's car suddenly, silently, appeared at the curb. Then he was standing before her, handsomer than she had remembered. For a breathless moment, neither of them could speak.

"Cherry—" Then he laughed quietly. "I—I was afraid, somehow, that you wouldn't be here."

"I'm here, Wade," she said softly.

Unfortunately at that moment Mr. Ames switched on the top light of the porch from the hall. He came out in the glare rattling a newspaper.

"Anyone seen the sports page?" he demanded loudly. "Oh, excuse me—"

Cherry could have cheerfully exiled her father to Patagonia. She wondered how he himself had ever been romantic enough to propose to her mother.

"Dad, this is Captain Wade Cooper of the Army Air Forces."

Wade did not seem to share her chagrin. In fact, he shook hands vigorously and seemed pleased to meet another man here.

"Awfully glad to know you, sir."

"So you're in the Air Forces. A pilot, eh? Our boy is, too. Well, we're very glad you're going to stay the week end with us."

"Good of you to have me, sir. Tell me, where is your son stationed?"

"Charlie's in the Pacific just now. He writes—"

Cherry cleared her throat. "Uh—don't you want to come in, Wade, and meet my mother?"

"Oh, sure, sure—just wait till I get my bag—"

Cherry's mother was a better accomplice than her father. Mrs. Ames had moved flowers and lamps and left all the double doors open between the several rooms to give an inviting vista. And she had dressed herself in her best black and pearls. She came forward to greet Wade warmly.

"We're delighted to have you visit us, Captain."

Wade looked at Mrs. Ames admiringly. "Thank you. I see your daughter takes after you for beauty, Mrs. Ames."

Cherry flushed with pleasure for herself and pride in her mother. Mrs. Ames signaled Cherry with a glance, "He's rather awkward but nice." Cherry barely perceptibly nodded back at her, amused, agreeing. Neither of the two men caught this little interchange.

"Have you had your dinner, Captain Wade? Are you sure?" Mrs. Ames was saying smoothly. "Because if you haven't, we can still serve you—"

There was a little commotion as Wade declined dinner and was told where his room was. Everyone stood chatting and getting acquainted a bit.

Mr. Ames started, "Well, sit down, Captain, and tell us something about—"

"Oh, Will, have you forgotten?" Mrs. Ames asked sweetly. "I particularly wanted to see that picture, and you promised—"

She turned graciously to Wade. "You'll excuse us, won't you? We'll have a good visit tomorrow."

Mr. Ames meanwhile looked perfectly blank, as if searching his mind for a promise he had never made. Cherry knew her parents had already seen that movie. But a stroll in the moonlight or a visit to the neighbors probably was what her mother had in mind.

With Mr. and Mrs. Ames headed for a movie or some other refuge, Cherry and Wade went back out on the porch. They settled into the porch swing. Moonlight shimmered all around them, the heavy sweetness of the earth permeated the night air.

"Nice here," Wade said softly. "Nice family you have, too."

"They *are* nice," Cherry reflected. Perhaps, since Wade considered her family an attraction, she should have persuaded her mother and father to stay home. Apparently Wade thought a nice family was an asset.

While she was thinking about this, Wade had inched closer. The swing, an old one, sagged perilously at their end. It said "Cre-e-e-eak" and as Wade started to murmur something, a voice said:

"Hello!"

It was Midge, sitting on the bottom porch step, invisible in shadow. She rose and came uninvited to sit in the swing with them, on Wade's other side.

"I hoped I'd get to meet you, Captain Wade," she said adoringly. "I've been watching for you from Pendleton's grape arbor across the street since six o'clock."

"You have, have you!" Cherry said sharply. Competition from Midge! It was funny but a nuisance.

"Yes, I have," Midge said innocently. She turned to the tall bronzed flier. "You know, Captain, I prefer older men."

Wade stared at the youngster in bobby socks. "Uh—don't you think you're a little young for—for this sort of thing? Of course, youth is fine—in fact, I'd considered *myself* young, until this minute—"

Cherry said hastily, "Besides, what about Tom Heaton?"

"Tom is very nice but he's a mere high school boy," Midge announced coolly.

"After all your labors—you're not interested in Tom now?" Cherry exclaimed.

"I've decided he's too young." Wade cleared his throat embarrassedly and Midge added, "I've just decided that."

"Well, I never! All along you've been palpitating over Tom!"

"I was behaving very youthfully, wasn't I? But a girl can learn a lot by—by meeting new people, can't she, Captain Wade? No, I want someone older—someone more—"

Wade choked. Cherry interrupted quickly.

"It was nice and friendly of you to come over, Midge. Good night, now."

"Ah—I—uh—" Midge said. Then she talked fast. "I have a perfectly fascinating book on flying, Captain Wade, you ought to see it, I'll bring it over tomorrow—"

"Good night, Midge!" Cherry said firmly.

Midge disappointedly stood up. "'Night." She trudged down the steps into the shadows. "And never mind that book about flying."

"Good night, Midge," Wade called, with a chuckle.

"Oh, yes! Good night to you, Captain Wade!" The girl waved and backed away as slowly as possible. It took her three minutes to get to the corner and turn it.

Then Wade laughed and put his hand over Cherry's. "Hello, pal," he said and kissed her.

"Hi," Cherry said. Wade's kiss was as friendly as a puppy dog's. He tugged her black curls into the bargain.

"Sure is good to see you," he said comfortably.

He gave a push with his foot and they went gently rocking in the swing.

"This is kind of different from the old days," Cherry sighed. "Remember?"

"I didn't travel all the way up here to talk over old times."

"You came to discuss the political situation," Cherry teased.

"I came to ask you to marry me," Wade said point-blank.

He stopped the swing. There was a moment's silence.

"Why, Wade," Cherry said. She could feel his arm about her trembling a bit. "I never dreamed you were serious."

He did not say anything, just looked at her.

"Why won't you believe I'm serious?" he demanded.

"Because—oh—you don't seem ready to settle down yet," Cherry said honestly. "You're awfully young and—and—I even wonder if you are genuinely in love with me! Or whether it's just—"

"Just what?" Wade was indignant.

"Well, you may be in love with love. Or in love with the general excitement of our war adventures together. Or in love with the springtime."

"Well, I like that!" Wade took his arm away and sat up very straight. "Boy tells girl he loves her and she won't believe him!"

"I know you from the old country," Cherry kidded him gently. "I know what a scapegrace you can be. I remember how you fell in and *out* of love with me. How you deserted me for a beautiful plane."

Wade ran his hands through his brown hair. "I'll prove to you I'm serious!" he exploded. "I'll make you believe me—" He waved his arms.

Cherry giggled in spite of herself. Wade looked more like an excited boy trying to hit a fly ball than a grown man ready to assume marriage and all its responsibilities.

"All right, Wade," Cherry said more quietly. "You prove to me if you can that you're serious about me and that you're ready to settle down in matrimony." She evaded his embrace and another giggle escaped her. "And I'll prove to you that you're *not!*"

"Agreed. How'll we start?" he said crossly.

"Haven't you any suggestions?"

Wade thought. "I'm dying to dance with you. But that isn't serious and sober enough, is it?"

"Well, what else?" Cherry's black eyes sparkled in the shadows.

"I thought it would be kind of fun to drive for miles and miles to nowhere in particular. The car's just humming. I've got gas," he said hopefully and then stiffened. "But I suppose having fun wouldn't prove I'm serious and settled."

"Haven't you one more little idea?"

Wade muttered, "Was going to buy us steaks and fixin's, after we'd danced all night and got good and hungry. But that won't prove to you—"

Cherry relented. "Wade, you old darling, those things sound wonderful! Let's do every one of them!"

"Honestly? All right! What are we waiting for?"

He pulled her out of the swing and into the car in a hop, skip and a jump. They went zooming down the moonlit street on two wheels, with Wade singing at the top of his voice.

The next day, Saturday, Cherry offered to put Wade to the most horrible test she could think of. She took him shopping.

They were both pretty tired from the evening before, which had been strenuous if not romantic. Cherry's feet ached from dancing and from Wade's stepping on them. Wade definitely had indigestion from having eaten in the middle of the night. He stood beside Cherry at the stocking counter, grumpy but determined, rehearsing the role of family man. Cherry almost felt ashamed of herself for teasing and doubting him. Maybe this impulsive boy was serious, at that.

"How do you like this color, Wade?"

"Lovely."

"Or this color?"

"Lovely." He yawned.

"Which color do you like best?"

"Both lovely. Heck, buy 'em all and let's get out of here."

Cherry paid for her stockings and marched him down the street to a grocery. She wandered around the vegetable stands, meditating over brightly colored squash, carrots, broccoli, tomatoes.

"What vegetables do you like, Wade?"

"I hate all vegetables."

"Well, which vegetables do you hate the least?"

"Spaghetti."

"A fine helpful cooperative husband you'd make! And a fine example you'd set the children, not eating your carrots."

Wade blinked. "What children?"

"Ours, of course."

Wade glanced around, down on the sawdust floor, as if expecting to see half a dozen toddlers or so. He grinned. "With me for a father, it'd be useless to try to make 'em eat carrots. Just feed 'em spaghetti."

It was Cherry's turn to blink. So Wade was handing her back her own blows.

The dry cleaning shop was next. Cherry waited while her cleaned raincoat was taken off the racks.

"Who takes your clothes to the cleaner's, Wade?" Cherry asked, thinking he would say he always took them himself.

"I dunno who takes my clothes over. I just leave them in my room on a chair or on the floor or somewhere, and sometime later they turn up hanging in my closet all cleaned and pressed. Surprise!"

"I guess that's the little brownies at work. Or your mother."

"I expect it's the brownies. Why?"

Cherry said primly, "Just curious about your sense of responsibility in small things."

"Listen, I'm so crazy about you, I'll take my own clothes to the cleaner's and yours too." He yawned again.

"If you remember."

"Aw, shucks. Don't do this to me. There's always the brownies."

Saturday lunch meant Mr. Ames was at home, too. The four of them had a pleasant visit over the meal. For once Velva was unobtrusive, except for pouring iced tea all over the tablecloth because she was staring so rapturously at Captain Cooper.

Lunch over, a sleepy, warm Saturday afternoon pall settled over the house and, indeed, over most of the town. The weather was not yet warm enough to go swimming. There was a ball game out at the Old Soldiers' Home but Wade, to Cherry's relief, did not want to go. Cherry called up the McClays to see if she and her guest could play on their tennis court, but the court was being rolled. That left the Golf Club, where Mr. Ames played not golf but bridge, and a walk through the woods, in the line of sports.

"Thumbs down," Wade decided. "Let's go out in the yard and loaf on the grass."

So they stretched out in the sun on the grass and watched a robin hopping around and indulged in the most luxurious sport of all: wasting time.

"Bored, dear?" Cherry asked wryly. "This is married life, y'know."

"Not bored a bit. I'm having a lovely time—Mrs. Cooper."

And they did have a lovely time, lazing away the long balmy afternoon. Wade talked to her for a while, but presently he fell asleep. Not long after, Cherry fell asleep too. They awoke full of ants and cricks in their backs and grass stains to find Mrs. Ames standing over them. Wade struggled politely to his feet.

"The McClays telephoned," she said. "They've just decided to have a party tonight and you two are invited."

"Nice," said Cherry. "I'll wear my new summer beige dress. It's regulation but it's come-hither silk."

Wade groaned. "Do we have to go to that party?"

"Married life, you know! Wife usually runs the family's social life."

Wade helped her to her feet muttering something about "this is a racket."

By eight-thirty that evening Cherry was freshly bathed, dressed, coifed, powdered and perfumed. The silk dress and highheeled slippers made her feel frivolous, keyed high for a lighthearted evening. She danced around the living room by herself to the music of the radio, waiting for Wade to appear in his dress uniform.

Mrs. Ames came in and put the evening paper on the table. "Where are Wade and your father?"

"Dad was lending Wade his electric razor and explaining its engineering principles, the last I heard," Cherry replied. "Madam, may I have this dance?" She held out an arm with exaggerated formality.

Mrs. Ames dropped a curtsy and said, "Charmed, Sir Percival, I'm sure." Cherry danced her mother around the living room until they were both out of breath and laughing.

"Oh, I can't wait for this party! Go-ing to a par-ty! Where is that Wade?" Cherry went to the foot of the stairs and whistled.

No answering whistle sounded.

"That boy is certainly taking a long time," Mrs. Ames obesrved. "Do you suppose he has locked himself into a closet, or fallen asleep again?"

"He's just primping." Cherry stood at the hall mirror and put a final pat of powder on her nose. Then she glanced at the paper. Then she halfheartedly listened to a radio program. By this time the clock's hand stood at nine o'clock.

Mrs. Ames called from upstairs, "Wade isn't anywhere up here. Nor Dad. You'd better go look for them."

As a posse of one, Cherry headed for the garage. There were the two men on their knees, tinkering around with machinery and talking. Cherry gingerly stepped over oil cans and avoided greasy rags, in her best clothes.

"Have you heard there is now a female of the species?" she inquired. "A new invention."

Wade and Mr. Ames looked up absent-mindedly.

"Oh, hello," Wade said. "You weren't waiting for me, were you?"

"No. Only giving an imitation."

"Well, you just run back to the house. Be right with you.

"That's right," Mr. Ames said soothingly. "You wouldn't want to get that pretty dress greased up out here."

Cherry made a short speech on the subject of social obligations but nevertheless had to retreat to the living room. She waited another fifteen minutes. The McClays telephoned. Cherry put more powder on her nose. Then she heard the sound of a car. She ran out to the porch in time to see her father and Wade drive off. They waved to her, maddeningly.

"Men!" Cherry fumed. "Men and machinery!"

Ten minutes later they pulled up to the curb.

"Terribly sorry," Wade said, bounding into the house. "I'll change—got oil on me—be right with you—"

He raced up the stairs, four steps at a time. Mr. Ames hastened after him.

"That razor ought to work now—I think we bought the right part for it—"

Cherry sat down alone in the living room and resigned herself. If they were going to repair the electric razor, she knew she would have a long wait. She had a very long wait. Mr. Ames made two more trips to the garage and back upstairs. Apparently they were fixing other things too, for Cherry heard hammering from above, and two interested masculine voices. The clock now said ten minutes to ten.

"At least," she thought disappointedly, "Wade is enjoying himself, even if I'm not."

At ten o'clock, Mrs. Ames told Cherry she was going to bed and read. At ten-fifteen, Wade leaned over the banister and called:

"You still down there, Cherry?"

"Yes," she answered in a small woebegone voice.

She heard her father and Wade in guilty whispering. Then Wade saying distinctly:

"Gosh, women are a responsibility, aren't they?"

At ten-forty, Cherry went to bed, angry, forlorn, and disgusted.

Sunday morning, Wade was only faintly triumphant and truly sorry.

"We'll have our own party," he promised. "That will be nicer, anyway, just you and I. We'll have a—a picnic, a grand one, since this is my last day in Hilton." He added gently, "And our last day together."

They would take his car, he said, and drive out to the loveliest meadow they could find. Wade insisted on going downtown and buying the picnic lunch at a restaurant, despite Mrs. Ames's offers. He brought little gifts for everyone, too, from the drugstore. "And I'll show you I can be romantic, Cherry. Forgiven?"

Cherry could hardly stay angry with a handsome young man whose brown eyes gleamed with mischief— who was trying so hard to please her.

It was a glorious day: they would picnic until the sun set. Actually they had been lazing in this peaceful meadow all afternoon, until now the sky was a fiery riot of red and gold, and their picnic lunch was still tucked in the basket.

Cherry spread out the cloth on the grass, as the sleepy birds twittered their last calls of the day. Wade was leaning against a tree trunk, watching her. The spreading oak made a leafy roof for them, a house of their own.

"This is what I mean, Cherry. If we could do these things together, always, for years and years."

"You mean not just playing," she said softly.

"I mean it." He came and sat down in the long rippling grass beside her. "Don't you see?"

Cherry almost saw, and believed, at that moment. Her hands trembled as she lifted food out of the basket. A lark sang one more song above them.

"Come eat your supper, Wade," she said gently, not knowing quite what else to say.

"No Midge, no relatives, no trivial distractions, now," Wade said pointedly. He filled a paper plate for her. He brought his sweater from the car's rumble seat and laid it over her shoulders against the cooling air.

They ate in dreaming silence. If this was love, Cherry thought, she wanted it, very much. Perhaps Wade was the one for her. Perhaps.

"There's one more thing I want to do, besides have you say yes," Wade said.

"What is it?"

"Go out on the water. There's a canoe on that river bank and a paddle. I don't think anyone would mind if we borrowed it for a little while, do you?"

Hand in hand they pushed through the deep grass and clover. Wade helped her down the crumbling bank, untied the fragile shell of canoe from a tree trunk, and they cautiously slid out onto the river.

Blueness was all around them—the high fading day blue overhead, the dark purple-blue of approaching evening lowering over the trees, the profound blue of the deep river.

Wade started to sing, not one of his usual ditties, but quietly, a love song four centuries old, stately and tender. His rich voice filled the song with his own feelings and echoed over the water:

> *"Drink to me only with thine eyes,*
> *And I will pledge with mine;*
> *Or leave a kiss but in the cup,*
> *And I'll not look for wine.*
> *The thirst that from the soul doth rise,*
> *Doth ask a drink divine—"*

Cherry could barely see his face in the gathering dusk. He could not see her either, for he was saying gently, "Cherry! Cherry—"

He rose and crawled forward in the canoe toward her, and lost his footing. The boat careened. They seized each other and the next second they were splashing, struggling, in the dark water.

"Cherry! Cherry! I'll get you! I'll save you!"

Cherry kicked furiously with her feet, and with one hand seized the paddle and sent it skimming toward the canoe. She swam to the overturned canoe, still treading water, and managed to force the canoe on its back.

Breathless, she looked around in the near-darkness for Wade.

He was thrashing wildly and going down.

Now she was really frightened. Wade was much bigger, heavier, than she was. His lashing arms struck her as she swam around him.

"Wade—Wade—lie still—stop fighting—!"

She dove under water, trying to grasp him about the waist, and lost him. All her Army nurse training came back to her, her muscles obeyed without her thinking. She dove again, found the choking flyer this time, and with a few mighty kicks got his head above water.

With one hand under his chin, she slowly swam toward shore, dragging Wade by floating him at her side. In knee-deep water he got to his feet and they walked onto the bank.

"Whew!" she sputtered. "Lie down, Wade, so I can pound your back and force some of that water out of your lungs."

"A fine thing—can't swim—ashamed of myself"—he coughed, as she gave him swimmer's first aid—"was going to save *you*!"

"Go back to the car and wrap yourself in everything dry and warm you can find!" she ordered and, kicking off her shoes, she splashed back into the water.

"Where are you going?" he wailed after her.

"To catch that canoe and paddle and tow them back!"

She had quite a struggle to find them in the dark. But they were light in weight, and Cherry took it slow and easy pushing them back. She would almost have enjoyed her swim, except that now here she stood at the car, dripping and bedraggled and her feet squishy in wet shoes. And except for the fact that Wade was highly insulted.

"A fine thing to do to me!" he stormed at her.

"Why, you ungrateful wretch, I saved your life!"

"A fine ending you tacked onto our romantic day!"

Cherry started to laugh. She laughed until she was staggering and gasping. The more she laughed the more infuriated Wade became.

He stalked around the car, a wretched, soggy figure of would-be dignity. "I certainly don't feel romantic about you now, Cherry Ames!" he shouted.

"—you unreasonable—Oh, you look so funny!"

"I wouldn't marry you now for anything!" he roared at her.

"Nobody asked you, sir, she said," Cherry retorted.

They drove back to town making puddles on the leather seat. Wade would not even speak to her. He looked straight ahead at the road all the way, as rivulets of water dripped from his flattened hair and ran off his nose.

At her house he let her out. His bag was already in the car.

"I've said good-bye to your parents," he said frigidly. "Good-bye to you, too." He let out the clutch with a savage jerk.

"Ah, Wade, don't be angry—come in and get dry—"

"Good-bye, you—you *lifesaver*! I'm going to marry a soft, helpless feminine little girl who'd let me drown!"

"There's your proof!" Cherry called after him. She dripped her way into the house still laughing. Apparently it wasn't love, after all. But it was fun!

It took a week for Wade to cool off. Then Cherry received this letter from him:

"You cured me of my romantic notions, all right. I guess you were right all along. But even though we aren't slated to be Papa and Mama, I can still foresee friendship for us. Can't you? Please forgive my stomping off, Cherry, and I'll be around to picnic with you sometime again. Wade.

"P.S. But not before I learn to swim."

CHAPTER XII

~~~~~~~~~~~~~~~~~~~~~~~~~~~~~~~~~

Strange Story

TOO MUCH TIME HAD ELAPSED SINCE CHERRY'S LAST visit to Toby. Try as she might, she had difficulty in finding free hours. Besides her eight hours of ward duty, she had errands to do for the men, extra hours at the canteen, lectures to attend, not to mention mending and shampoos.

"If only I didn't have to waste time eating and sleeping!" Cherry thought.

Finally Sal came to her rescue again. Sal was always willing to work extra hours, so Cherry might go to her small audience of one.

It was raining this afternoon as Cherry walked through the Demarest grounds. The rain was warm and sweet-smelling, and burst open the buds on bush and hedge. Perhaps Toby would be well enough to come outdoors into this garden some fine day very soon.

But Grace Demarest's face gave Cherry a shock. Toby's young mother looked today as she had when Cherry first met her: strained, hiding anxiety behind a false calm. Mr. Demarest was not around. The house was empty of visitors and unusually quiet.

"How is Toby?" Cherry asked without preliminaries.

Mrs. Demarest shook her head. "He's not well, my dear. Not well at all."

"But he was so improved just a short time ago—"

"Dr. Orchard told us it would not last. Toby is slipping back again—going back, and back, and back, to where he was."

"But it's so sudden." Cherry thought if Toby had really been built up, the child could hold his ground a little longer than this. He had not really been built up, then. He had been depending on some medicine or drug, and apparently that drug had reached its saturation point in his system and could no longer help.

She ached all over for this sad woman beside her. But there was no use in offering theories or asking questions. That would only upset Mrs. Demarest more.

"Is Toby well enough for me to see him?" Cherry asked. "If he isn't, I'll come back another day."

"Another day he will only be that much weaker, I'm afraid. Let's go upstairs. He has been asking for you."

Cherry was shocked when she saw the little boy. He still showed traces of having been stronger and livelier than before this strange treatment. But he was a paler, more listless little boy than Cherry had expected to see. It was not his condition today, so much as the warning it showed, that terrified Cherry. Toby's health was coasting downhill again. As a nurse she recognized the danger signs. And she knew that, at this rate, Toby would rapidly be approaching the very bottom of his endurance.

"Cherry, where was you?" Toby smiled up at her, teasing. "I bet you forgot any more stories."

"Oh, I still know dozens of stories, you rascal! But I guess you don't want to hear any more stories."

"Do too." He leaned forward eagerly but the effort exhausted him. He seemed surprised and dizzy, and his mother had to lay him back against the pillows. He repeated in a whisper, "You forgot the stories! Ha ha!"

"Now don't try to talk, dear, and Cherry will tell you a story."

Cherry chose a gentle and fanciful one: the legend of the three Moorish princesses who lived in Spain, in the southern hill town of Granada, in the castle called the Alhambra. "They were three young sisters, and their names were Zaida, Zorayda, and Zorahayda."

"Pretty names," the child breathed. His little hand in hers was cold, despite the warm day and his blankets.

"They were very lonely and unhappy locked up in the castle, and they had three Spanish lovers who asked them to run away." Cherry recounted Washington Irving's resplendent tale—the escape of the eldest by night, the galloping horses, the crossing at the river. "Then the second sister decided she too would climb down from the high balcony, down the steep, dangerous hillside, to where her lover waited with swift horses." And finally the tale was told, with the dutiful youngest sister left behind, to mourn her loneliness.

"She still sings and plays her dulcimer in the fountains at the Alhambra, and if you go there at night, and are very quiet, she will appear in the fountain in all her gorgeous raiment, and tell you her sad story."

"And the mean old lady guardian got drownded in the river," Toby repeated with relish. "Served her right. Served the mean old father right, too. Huh!"

His mother laughed softly. "Such indignation, Toby!"

He seemed satisfied, but so tired, his blue eyes were so heavy, that Cherry decided to go.

"I'll come back tomorrow and tell you the most wonderful story yet," she promised, looking down at him tenderly.

"Don't go 'way," he pleaded. "Please don't go 'way. Tomorrow is far off. Maybe it'll never get to *be* tomorrow."

Cherry swallowed hard. Did the little fellow guess how unlikely his own tomorrows were? She avoided looking at his mother.

"Aw, Cherry, please stay. Please!"

She sat down again. All the old feeling of helplessness surged through her, to see his life trickling away. She remembered once going into a hospital kitchen and seeing a bottle of milk lying on its side where it had fallen over on the table. Most of the milk had already run out of the bottle. Cherry had stood there fascinated, watching the rest of the milk gurgle out in a small, slow, deliberate stream, slower and slower as the last remaining drops slid away, one by one, and the bottle was empty. That was the way life was slipping out of Toby's small, starving body.

Stifling a sob, Cherry hastily excused herself and went quickly out of the room. On the landing, she almost collided with Toby's nurse. Her eyes brimming with tears, Cherry searched the nurse's face for signs of hope and encouragement regarding her little patient's condition. The nurse shook her head slowly, "Poor little tyke!" she said. "If only Dr. Orchard could get some more of that wonderful medicine. It did the trick. But he can't, it seems."

"What medicine?" Cherry wanted to know.

"I don't know," the nurse was brusque in her reply. "Please, Lieutenant," she begged, "don't mention what I said to anyone." A worried look crossed her face.

"But why?" Cherry demanded to know. "Why do you ask me not to mention it to anyone?"

The nurse by now was almost frantic. "Please, Lieutenant, don't ask me any more questions. Dr. Orchard asked me not to discuss this case with anyone—and he's my superior. I must go back to my duties, now." She almost ran in her haste to get away.

Cherry puzzled over the conversation she just had had, as she walked slowly back to the little boy's bedroom and sat down. While Mrs. Demarest was quietly talking to Toby, Cherry's mind was in a whirl. Why should Dr. Orchard be so secretive about his technique? Why had he evaded answering her when she had asked him what medicines or drugs he used, to have so remarkably improved Toby's condition—and with such an obviously weak answer, too? What was this special medicine which the nurse was not to mention? And why couldn't he get any more of it? *Special medicine.* Suddenly a thought struck her. Thinking back quickly, she remembered Toby had shown signs of improvement immediately after the robbery at the hospital. Could it have been those stolen amino acid medicines that had improved Toby so miraculously?

"It all seems to tie up!" Cherry exclaimed aloud.

"What did you say, my dear?" Mrs. Demarest asked.

"I said, I'd like to stay and see Dr. Orchard today. If you don't mind."

"Certainly, stay."

"An' tell me a story," Toby said.

Cherry started another story, telling it absent-mindedly. She was occupied with a flood of questions about this clue she had just discovered. Chiefly: should she, had she any right, to follow a clue if it might mean closing off the source of Toby's cure? How was she to balance the theft of the medicine needed for her soldiers versus the pathos of this little boy, the heartbreak of his parents?

"That's not a very good story," Toby said, with justice.

"I'm sorry, dear. I—"

"Tell me about the mean old lady getting drownded again."

Cherry started once more on the story of the Moorish princesses, and was getting a fine, vengeful response from her small listener when Dr. Orchard arrived.

He seemed tired this afternoon, a little discouraged too.

"Hello, Mrs. Demarest. Oh, hello, Miss Ames. Well, Toby, are you in a better humor now than you were this morning?"

Toby sulked up at him in silence.

"Dr. Orchard is coming twice a day now," Mrs. Demarest said to Cherry. She added half jokingly, "We'd be glad to have him move right in, if that would facilitate his work."

"Thank you, but it's not so simple as that."

"If there is anything we can do—purchase for you—medicines, instruments—"

"The one thing I'd like to have, Mrs. Demarest, is not to be had for love or money," he said.

"What is that?" Mrs. Demarest asked, and Cherry too was listening intently.

"Oh—" The plump young doctor laughed a bit. "Luck, I suppose. A little luck and more strength for this young man."

Cherry thought, the stolen amino acid medicines cannot be purchased. Not anywhere, not for any sum, because they are still Army property, and still secret, not yet perfected. Other medicines, even other amino types, yes, but not these particular ones! She knew the Army Medical Corps did not want that medicine to get out. The hospital authorities had regarded the theft as a very serious blow. Luck, Dr. Orchard said he needed. Luck, indeed! Those special amino acid medicines were what he needed—unless Cherry's reasoning was very wrong.

Cherry asked Dr. Orchard a question, phrasing it with care, to get the kind of answer she sought.

"Dr. Orchard, it's correct, isn't it, to assume that part of your treatment for Toby was a beneficial medicine?"

"Why, yes, naturally."

Suddenly, giving him no warning, no time to get on guard, Cherry stated:

"And now you've run out of that medicine and need more."

"Yes, I—" He started, checked himself. Fear came into his pale eyes.

Mrs. Demarest said innocently, "I do hope you'll let us order more of it immediately."

"I was going to give you a prescription for it this afternoon," Dr. Orchard said. He took out his prescription pad and wrote. Cherry recognized the abbreviated Latin formula: it was a simple, common medicine, obtainable at any drugstore. Dr. Orchard looked at Cherry triumphantly, as he handed the slip of paper to Mrs. Demarest.

Cherry was not fooled. She knew this was not the medicine that had revived Toby's assimilative powers. But she kept a bland face and let Dr. Orchard believe he had allayed her suspicions. Dr. Orchard had unwittingly confirmed those suspicions! Now she was ready to leave.

For the rest of that day, Cherry could think of nothing else. Again and again, she reviewed all the different little incidents that had led up to her belief that Dr. Orchard might have used the stolen amino drug on Toby. Step by step, over and over again—first, the robbery, then Toby's miraculous improvement so soon after the robbery, Dr. Orchard's evasion of her questions about his technique, and Toby's relapse, the strange behavior of the nurse on the case, and finally Dr. Orchard's writing of the prescription for a simple, common medicine obtainable at any drugstore. All these incidents seemed to connect in Cherry's mind to form the one word—GUILTY!

Again and again she asked herself how, if he had used the stolen drug, had he accomplished the robbery? How could he have managed it? He had no access even to the hospital grounds, much less to an inner sanctum like the medical storeroom.

Or did he have an accomplice within the hospital? Not likely, Cherry thought. She had seen him with hospital people here at the Demarests', but in every case, Dr. Orchard had only the slightest acquaintance with any of the hospital people. His practice, his personal life, so far as she knew, touched their lives almost not at all. Cherry was stumped.

But of one thing she was certain. If Dr. Orchard had used the stolen amino drug, he would probably try to go on using it—and there would be a second robbery from the medical storeroom!

Cherry resolved to keep her eyes and ears wide open, to watch for the warning moment.

She was in the ice-cream parlor with Sal Steen two evenings later. Somehow the gossipy atmosphere of the place set Sal to talking.

"The Demarest boy is worse. I was over there this afternoon. Wish you could get over tomorrow. He's so thin it's pathetic. His parents look like ghosts. Cherry, I've been wondering if those new amino acid medicines we know so little about might help save him. Of course we really don't know about that special type the Army has. And I suppose they've tried everything."

Cherry held her tongue. If she were wrong, it would be bad enough to get herself in trouble, without involving Sal too. "It's a shame. It seems terrible enough when anyone dies, but when a little four-year-old drifts away like this—" She thought of young Mr. and Mrs. Demarest, who were so friendly and generous, and how they felt. "Just Dr. Orchard, the local doctor, is on the case now," she reminded Sal.

"Speak of the devil—there's your Dr. Orchard. Coming in." Sal said incredulously, "Is that Margaret Heller coming in with him?"

Both girls stared. But the plump young doctor sat down alone at one table and Margaret Heller joined some women in a booth.

"I don't like him," Cherry admitted to Sal.

"You don't like him for the same reason nobody likes him, much, that is. He's so blamed ambitious and conceited and sort of cold. He's just out to make himself a big medical reputation."

"Well, I hope he can save the Demarest child," Cherry replied.

"It would certainly boost him to fame if he could."

Margaret Heller smiled stiffly as Cherry and Sal passed her booth on their way out. She certainly is a prim-looking person, Cherry thought. She looks about as efficient and appealing as a set of typewriter keys.

In Nurses' Quarters, Cherry said good night to Sal and went into her own room. Instead of going to bed, she restlessly wandered around the room. Far in the back of her mind she was thinking. But she could not dredge up these half-formed feelings, these obscure bits of ideas, into clear, definite thoughts. All she knew was that she distrusted Dr. Orchard. Her mind ticked away, singing a song she could not decipher.

"There must be an answer," Cherry thought impatiently. "There must be."

CHAPTER XIII

Midnight Discovery

GOOD NEWS CAME TO CHERRY ONE BRIGHT MORNING. The redoubtable Principal Chief Nurse had rated her performance "worth while" and elevated Cherry to be in charge of Orthopedic Ward.

Cherry was gratified but not excited about being chief nurse of the ward. Her work continued very much what it had been. Only now she had the responsibility of the ward, the paper work to do, visits to make to the X-ray and fluoroscope rooms. She had to watch that the other three nurse-lieutenants gave penicillin to the proper patients at exactly three-hour intervals, and she made the rounds of the patients morning and afternoon with the doctor. But Cherry still had time for play.

As Jim said, "It's not only good care but having someone around when we need to talk, or could use a laugh."

This warm afternoon Cherry had brought several of the advanced patients out on the hospital lawn. Established on blankets thrown over the grass, or in wheel chairs, Cherry then gave them milk and cookies.

"Quite an outing," George approved. He held his milk in his left hand and managed the cookie with a metal hooklike contraption that served as his right hand. The hook did the job. George wore it openly, not ashamed, trusting other people to understand.

Redheaded Matty in his shortened cast and wheel chair grumbled good-humoredly as usual. "Look at them guys! Where're they going with the fishing rods! Not to drink milk, I bet!" He pointed.

"All right, one of the corpsmen will take you fishing tomorrow," Cherry promised. "Since that's what your little heart desires."

The ex-cowboy looked placated. "But you won't make me eat the fish, you understand. I can't stomach fish."

"Maybe you won't catch any," Jim suggested. He was slowly, swayingly, walking around the grass on his new steel-and-leather leg. He used no cane or crutches, either. Hy Leader said all Jim needed was a parasol to look like a tightrope walker. "Go climb a tree," Jim told Hy pleasantly. "I'll be on the soft ball team before you are."

Cherry asked, "Are you going to join the Sod Busters or the Ruptured Ten?"

"Lady," said Ralph Pernatelli, "the Ruptured Ten is a very fine outfit. I would join them myself if I didn't have better things to do with my healing arm." For Ralph's arm was now out of the cast and he had made a discovery. In Occupational Therapy, Ralph had progressed from molding clay to the finer work of molding delicate silver wire into jewelry. His healing hand produced things of such beauty that Ralph was elated. "I'd like to make this my lifework," he had told Cherry. "I used to be an insurance salesman, but that job never seemed to have anything to do with *me*. But designing and making jewelry—well, I've found *my* work!"

So Cherry had taken him to the Educational Reconditioning people here at the Army hospital. They were giving Ralph professional training. Ralph was sitting here on the grass with Cherry and his wardmates reluctantly, and only because the silversmithy was closed for the day. Cherry felt very proud of him, and proud of the progress all "her" men had made.

"Loo-tenant Ay-yums!" A lanky figure in a seersucker dress came loping toward them. It was Sal Steen, and she filched a cookie on her way. "Hi, fellows. My compliments, Nurse. Is there a mechanic in your midst? A typewriter in the main office broke down and they can't find anyone to fix it."

Jim looked eagerly at Cherry. "I believe I could repair it. Miss Cherry. It's quite a long walk for my empty foot, but I see you brought my crutches just in case—"

"Certainly, go ahead, Sergeant," Cherry said. For Jim to work with his hands was good therapy. And for him to help someone else would further strengthen his growing self-confidence. "Do you know where it is?"

"Sure, the star-shaped building." He went off alone, quite proudly.

Sal said aside to Cherry, "What's doing on your ward?"

"Oh, penicillin, dressings. Have some new arrivals." Cherry said softly, "They are almost breaking my heart. Just as these boys did at the beginning."

"I know. The best part is seeing the patients get well, the worst part is seeing the helplessness of the fellows." Sal dipped into the cookies again and called, "Don't let Ames boss you around too much. Well, so long, kids."

"Well, so long, kids," Hy Leader mimicked her, and started hopping away.

"And where are you off to?" Cherry demanded. "Gosh, if I didn't boss you, you rascals would run off with the hospital."

Hy explained that he was going to rehearsal. "'Course, Public Relations is bringing in a Broadway show but the GIs love my act."

"Wait a minute, Iron Man, I'm not staying around here with these cripples." Bailey Matthews vigorously wheeled his chair after Hy. He looked more like a halfback than an invalid. "I'm going over to *The Goldbrick* office to get a copy of our local talent magazine."

Hy and Matty went down the path together, helping each other along. Cherry turned to George and Ralph, and grinned.

"That leaves only us. Would you mind going back to the ward now? One of the new fellows is coming down from O.R. and I promised him I'd be there when he wakes up."

Cherry had been back on the ward only long enough to take care of the operative case, and rig up a fork-holding wand for a soldier with badly burned, bandaged hands, when Jim returned.

Cherry had never seen Jim Travers like this. He was furiously angry. He hobbled rapidly past her to his own bed and hurled his crutches on the floor.

"For heaven's sake, Jim! That man's ill—be quiet!"

"Sorry." Jim reached over and turned off a radio that was softly playing. "Sorry." But his face was still taut with rage. He bit out, "Who is that woman named Heller?"

"Miss Heller? What about her?"

"Come out here in the hall."

Cherry finished what she was doing and followed the tense patient to the corridor. He told her a curious story.

He arrived at the typing and file room to find that all the office staff had gone home for the day. Only Miss

Heller, the office supervisor, was there. She had shown him the broken typewriter. Jim sat down, looked it over, worked on it a bit, and had said:

"I can't fix it without tools. Have you a screw driver or a pair of pliers?"

Margaret Heller had looked at him with scorn. Then she sat down and fixed the typewriter herself—using nothing but her fingers.

Jim said to Cherry, "It was quite a feat. I'll never forget her toollike fingers! Such a mousy little woman and she repaired that typewriter better than a man—you'd never expect it from the looks of her!"

Cherry asked curiously, "If she could fix it herself all along, why did she send for a repairman?"

"Beats me. If I were as expert as she is, I wouldn't keep it a secret."

"Hmm. It's funny—But what are you sizzling about, Jim? Not jealous of her?"

"No, though I certainly admit she's good. Well, when she finished fixing the typewriter—"

Margaret Heller had smugly sat there and looked Jim over from head to foot. She realized how amazed he was at what she had just accomplished. And she had sneered at him: "I don't see why you couldn't fix it, anyone could, it's simple. You at least have two *hands!*"

"I won't forget her in a hurry," Jim said between his teeth to Cherry. "Not after a remark like that!" He hit the wall with his clenched fist. "Oh, why did she have to remind me I'm a cripple!"

"Jim, stop that!" Cherry said sharply.

"I hate that Margaret Heller," Jim muttered. "That job *wasn't* simple. I'll never forget her."

Cherry said nothing but she, too, bitterly resented what Margaret Heller had done to her patient. Of all the ugly, demoralizing things to say! To set a wounded man back!

In the days that followed Cherry was constantly on the alert for any warning signs of a second robbery of the storeroom, in spite of the many tasks to be done that crowded her days to the full! They were pleasant tasks: helping arrange an exhibit of the decorative metalwork, woodwork, printing, sculpture, painting, model ships and planes, radios, new inventions the men had made—prying Matty out of his cast and putting him temporarily into a leather halter which he declared made him feel like a saddled horse—assisting the ex-soldiers to arrange their souvenirs of Bank of France notes, German helmets, Sicilian pottery, Japanese battle flags, cathedral pictures from Casablanca, in good order to take home.

In addition, two wonderful men—almost wizards—came to the hospital. One was a famous teacher of ballroom dancing, who swore any of the legless boys could dance. They did not believe him at first. But he picked Jim Travers and, with some instruction and encouragement, Jim was dancing up and down the aisle of beds with Cherry, to the records the man had brought. All the men clamored for dancing lessons, then. Their visitor smiled and wrote out scholarships for all of them, at his dancing schools in or near their home cities.

The other man was smiling, stocky, and modest. He was known all over America as the finest make-up artist for Hollywood movie stars. "Now watch," he told them. He took a handsome new arrival, easily the handsomest man in the whole hospital, and made him up as a gnome. He looked so ugly that Cherry and the others could hardly believe their eyes. "Now watch this," said the make-up artist. He selected the Orphan, at whom no one had ever tossed an admiring glance. He combed the Orphan's hair a different way, pasted on a slender mustache, tied a plaid muffler under his chin, and handed him a good-looking walking stick. Result: the Orphan's limp became fascinating and the Orphan himself dashing!

"You see?" said the artist. "You can look well, every one of you. I'll show you how." And he convinced the wounded young men that it was possible to turn a liability into an asset.

Morale raisers like these cheered up Cherry, too. But the incident about Margaret Heller and Jim depressed her, and the worsening condition of Toby whom she could not get out of her mind.

MIDNIGHT DISCOVERY

Only today she had received a message from Mrs. Demarest. It was a cryptic message, in answer to a telephone inquiry Cherry had made about Toby. One of the corpsmen took it over the phone.

"Tell Miss Cherry Toby's condition is worse, but that the doctor promises a quick improvement."

Cherry had read that note on her ward with a hard-beating heart. Toby worse! And Dr. Orchard promising, actually, that he would show a quick improvement. This, then, was her warning moment! This said clearly that, if there were to be a second robbery, it would be soon. *Now!*

All that afternoon, Cherry worked on her ward with only part of her mind on her job. The rest of her thoughts were on her instant, reckless decision. She knew without thinking what she was going to do. She had no right to do it. It was properly no concern of hers. But she was going to stand watch tonight at the medical storeroom, and as many nights as necessary, during the still hours when few people were around.

There was a night watchman, of course, for the building which housed the storeroom. But he was an old man, and all alone in a large building. Cherry had heard that after the robbery, a special guard was posted at the storeroom. But there had been a subsequent whisper that the hospital authorities were relying on special locks more than on guards.

Whoever was posted there, whatever the circumstances, did not matter to Cherry. Not after this phone message from Mrs. Demarest! She would go! Alone, if necessary—for who would go with her? What could she tell anyone, anyway? She had no evidence, no proof, only suspicions. Was there anyone who shared her suspicions? She thought not.

The evening of Mrs. Demarest's warning message, Cherry was in the village with Jim. They had come in after supper at the hospital, to search for a strip of special satiny wood to inlay a fine handkerchief box Jim was making. Cherry suspected the box was intended for herself. They found the wood in one of the shops, and since it was still light, went for a stroll. Cherry wanted Jim to have as much practice walking as possible. The leafy trees and gardens in yards invited them down residential side streets.

"Funny old Victorian houses," Jim commented, as they slowly walked along.

"Funny old broken sidewalks," Cherry countered. "How are you making out?"

"Perfectly all right. Say, look at that house with all the wooden curlicues around the roof. Gingerbread!"

"Look at that shabby one with all the doodads on the porch," Cherry pointed out, and caught herself.

Margaret Heller was on that porch, standing before the closed door. Cherry preferred Jim not to see her:

MIDNIGHT DISCOVERY 183

Heller could upset him. But Jim had seen, and stood there galvanized with hatred.

"Come on," Cherry urged. "There's an interesting house up farther."

But still Jim did not move.

Margaret Heller, they saw, was fumbling in her handbag. Obviously this was her house, and just as obviously she had forgotten her key. She rang the doorbell and waited. Miss Heller rattled the doorknob. Then they saw her take a hairpin from her hair. She tinkered with the lock. In about half a minute she had the door open. She went in and disappeared.

"Jim!" Cherry whispered. "Jim! This rings a bell in my mind! She picked that lock—what was it? Wait—what?—"

Cherry bent her head and closed her eyes. Sal Steen's voice floated back in her memory: "That lock was *picked*."

Picked. The lock of the medical storeroom, from which the medicines had been stolen.

Cherry saw it all fit together now! Margaret Heller went all over the hospital quite naturally, delivering office directives, picking up reports. She could go anywhere in the hospital without question. She had keys, too—and Cherry remembered the outer door to the medical storeroom had been locked and opened by a key. That settled it!

"What's wrong?" Jim demanded. He was looking very puzzled.

Cherry took a deep breath and decided to confide in him. Jim, after his experiences with Heller, would believe her. She would need help, for what she planned to do. Jim would willingly help her, and he could be trusted.

"Jim, you must have heard about the medicines being stolen—" She told him the entire story. "I checked and learned there is no special guard there—only the night watchman. But there are special locks! And if Heller can open locks—"

Cherry brought herself up short. She knew how serious it is, how dangerous, to accuse unjustly. She was determined to secure proof. "Jim, we have to do something! Tonight!"

As a staff nurse, and particularly as chief nurse of a ward, Cherry had the right to go to the medical storeroom. To keep watch there between ten and twelve—the likeliest hours that Heller would come—and to take a patient with her, was stretching her rights a bit. But the night watchman downstairs did not challenge her.

"This is dangerous going. Think it's worth while?" Jim asked, as they climbed the stairs in the quiet, echoing building.

"Don't you?"

"Yes. I surely would like to catch the thief in the act."

MIDNIGHT DISCOVERY

It was ten o'clock. They took up posts in the darkened storeroom. The room was utterly black, the rooms leading into it were dark too. They sat on wooden chairs before the various metal compartments, within range of both the locked door and the locked compartment containing the amino acid medicines. Jim kept his hands deep in his pockets, so the glowing radium dial of his wrist watch would not gleam. They did not talk, and scarcely breathed, ears straining for every sound. After eleven o'clock, the voices on the paths and from the other buildings died down. All they heard occasionally was the watchman moving around downstairs in the lobby, now and then the ghostly snappings of beams and floor boards.

There was a faint scratching at the door. Cherry seized Jim's arm. Nothing happened at the door. It might have been only a mouse.

The scratching started again, lasted the briefest moment. Then the faintest of clicks, recognizable as a key turning. The door softly opened, closed. A figure slid over the floor, soundless. No flashlight. Cherry and Jim literally held their breaths. The figure stopped before the amino acids compartment, within their hands' grasp. It was so dark they could not see who it was—someone in a tightly buttoned coat, head muffled in the collar. It sickeningly struck Cherry that it might be a professional thief, and with a gun—not Heller at all!

Faint scratching started again. It stopped, started, scratched and grated softly. Then the figure's hand went to its head and next they heard the pianissimo tap of metal on metal. A hairpin!

Cherry sprang up and switched on the lights.

Margaret Heller cowered there, the compartment door swung open, the packet of medicine in her hand.

"Watchman!" Cherry shouted. "Watchman!"

Margaret Heller broke toward the door but Jim seized her. He nearly fell down and Cherry joined the struggle. The two wooden chairs fell over.

"Let me go!" the prim woman panted. "Let me go!"

But Cherry had a strong grip on her.

"You can't deny this!" she exclaimed. "Not with two witnesses!"

"It's not my fault!" Margaret Heller gasped out. Her face was stark white, pinched with cowardice. "*He* made me do it!"

"He? Who?"

"Oh, I'm not going to protect him. Dr. Orchard—he's the one—"

She tried suddenly to wrench away but Jim and Cherry held her.

"All right. All right." Her face and voice were hateful. "Dr. Orchard wanted to try this medicine on the Demarest boy. He paid me to get it for him. I knew it was wrong but I—well, I like Dr. Orchard, he takes me out sometimes, we meet in the next town. I wanted him to like me—"

The watchman came running in, and Cherry was glad to see two of the doctors with him. One of them telephoned to the Principal Chief Nurse.

Jim had not said a word in all this time. There was no gloating or revenge in his face. He looked profoundly disgusted, and tired.

"So that," he said clearly to Cherry, "is that. Now let's get out of here."

There was nothing Cherry could say, either. She felt only loathing, and was relieved to get away and into the cool, clean night air.

CHAPTER XIV

The Happiest Day

THE AFTERMATH OF CATCHING THE THIEF LEFT CHERRY with some oddly mixed reactions.

The best part of it was that, a few days later, Jim received a private citation for his part in the affair. What had taken place, that night, was not publicized around the hospital. Very few people knew there even had been a second, attempted theft. But at a quiet ceremony in the general's office, Jim was congratulated on his courage and handed a letter from Washington, praising him and thanking him. The honor, and the exploit itself, put the crowning touch on Jim's rebuilt confidence. Cherry was very happy about him.

Cherry too received a commendation. She was pleased, but much more concerned about Toby. Now that she had stopped Heller from supplying Dr. Orchard with the amino acid medicine, what would become of Toby? Cherry could and must do one thing.

Screwing up all her courage, Cherry went to see Colonel Brown after duty hours. The Principal Chief Nurse let her sit in the outer office long enough to get thoroughly jittery. Then she consented to receive her. The small white-haired colonel glared at Cherry as severely and impatiently as ever and said:

"Well? What is it?"

"It's about the stolen medicine—well, in a way—it's about Toby, the little boy Dr. Orchard was treating."

"Toby!" the colonel almost snorted. "Lieutenant Ames, I'm concerned with military patients only. I have no time to discuss civilian cases," she snapped, dismissing Cherry with a brusque wave of her hand.

"But, Colonel Brown, just one more moment," Cherry begged.

"I've given you all the time I can spare. Good day, Lieutenant Ames." It was a curt and final dismissal.

Cherry's temper flared up at the coldness, the callousness of this woman. "I'll be darned," she thought, "if I'll let her throw me out. Not with Toby's life at stake!" Aloud she said, her black eyes flashing, and her cheeks hotly flushed:

"I'm sorry to intrude on you, Colonel Brown, but I must stay until you answer a crucial question."

"Oh, indeed! Lieutenant Ames."

"Yes, ma'am, I must!" Cherry countered stubbornly.

Unexpectedly, Colonel Brown looked amused. So she liked people to stand up to her! "All right," she said more amenably, and actually sat down at her desk to listen. "What is it?"

Cherry's words came tumbling out. She reminded the Principal Chief Nurse of all that Toby's parents had done for the soldier patients—of their generosity and unselfishness even in the face of their own tragedy. She pleaded with the colonel to secure the authorization to release the amino medicines for the little boy. "If you only will, Colonel Brown! There is no other way to get it for him—and without it—"

"You plead a beautiful case, Lieutenant Ames." And to Cherry's amazement, there was a twinkle in the fierce little nurse's eyes. "For your information, I have already applied for, and have received the authorization. Toby will have his medicine. All he needs. And now, Lieutenant Ames, the door out is there."

"Thank you very—"

"Don't stop to thank me! Can't you see I'm busy?"

Cherry fled, laughing to herself, and happy. What a relief! Toby would have the essential medicine! That old crosspatch—but she wasn't such an old crosspatch after all—would get the medicine to Toby without delay too. Now Toby would be cured!

She raced to a phone booth and called the Demarest home. The butler answered. "Tell Mr. and Mrs.

Demarest that Lieutenant Ames has wonderful news for them—and will be right over!"

Bill and Grace Demarest were waiting for her on the road at the bus stop. Their drawn faces tensed still more as she ran up to them.

"Cherry, what is it? It's about Toby, isn't it?"

"Yes! Yes! Yes!" Cherry sang out. "Toby is to get that medicine—right away—for as long as he needs it! The Army Medical Corps will supply it!"

The two Demarests burst into confused, happy words. Mrs. Demarest clung to Cherry's arm, hardly knowing what she was saying.

"Toby will live, now! He'll live! Our little boy—!"

A horn honked as a staff car pulled up. In it sat Colonel Brown, stiff as a ramrod, her face severe, her visored hat on askew in her hurry. In her lap was a parcel. The medicine!

"I've come to investigate this case myself and secure verification of the facts, Lieutenant Ames. Where are the Demarests?"

"We're Toby's parents, Colonel," Mr. Demarest said. "If you'll be good enough to drive up to our house and come in—"

"Get in, get in! Hurry up, I'm a busy woman."

Cherry came as near to hugging the fierce little nurse, at that moment, as anyone probably had ever done.

At the house, Cherry left the Demarests with the colonel in the living room—not risking the colonel's curt dismissal. Besides, she could not wait to see Toby, on this day of days!

The little boy's pallor and weakness did not hurt her today as before. Now Toby would be not traveling downhill, but marching uphill to health. Now his present pitiful condition would be only a yardstick by which to measure his sure, lasting recovery. Of all the days she had visited Toby, this was the happiest day.

"H'lo, Cherry. Your cheeks are awful red. Like a napple."

"Like red cherries," his nurse smiled. "I'll leave you two old cronies together." She closed the door behind her.

Cherry sat down in her usual place by Toby's bed. Her black eyes danced at him. "Want to hear the happiest story I ever told you yet?"

"Yes!"

"All right. Once upon a time there was a little boy who was sick—"

"Like me?"

"Just like you. In fact, his name was Toby."

Toby began to smile. "Was he a nice little boy?"

"An extremely nice little boy. Everybody liked him. He—"

"Was this Toby—was he me?"

"Well, that's for you to decide—when we get to the end of the story."

Cherry's story version of the illness was much merrier than it had been in fact. There were imaginary doctors in the shape of birds and elephants mixed up in it, who tried to cure the small patient with peanuts and flying lessons from the branch of a tree. There were also, on demand, cops and robbers whom the storied Toby dealt with mightily.

"Never mind the elephants and robbers any more," Toby decided. "Tell me about did the little boy get well?"

"Yes, he did get well. Quickly, too. And he stayed well."

"An' did he go to a circus?"

"To a circus, and to school with the other children, and swimming and hiking, and he grew up to be a strong man."

Toby listened with merriment in his very blue eyes. "I'm not a grown-up man *yet*."

"Oho, who said the little boy in the story was you?"

"Yes, it is. You can't fool me. It's the same Toby who gets well!"

Cherry nodded, smiling, and he nodded his head in time with hers.

"Now isn't that the best story I ever told you?"

He asked her soberly, "Am I really going to get well?"

"Yes, darling, you are."

He sighed and turned over on the pillows, thinking. Presently he reached out and tried to pull Cherry's rosy face down to his.

"What is it, Toby?"

"I want to kiss you on account of you tell me all those stories."

He planted a large, noisy, fervent kiss on her cheek. "Now you kiss me too."

Cherry obliged, with feeling.

"Now you rest," she said. "Because getting well is a job, and you have to work at it."

He closed his eyes tightly. "A' right, I'm resting."

Cherry tiptoed away from the bed.

"Will I be all well tomorrow?"

"Not tomorrow, but soon—if you rest now."

"Like Toby in the story." He screwed up his eyes again and snuggled contentedly into the covers.

Cherry had to pause on the upper landing and blink the happy tears out of her eyes. Then she went on downstairs, to join the Demarests in the living room.

Colonel Brown was in the music room, talking to someone. Mrs. Demarest had unashamedly been crying.

"We don't know how to thank you, Cherry," Mr. Demarest said.

"There's nothing to thank me for," she said honestly. "Thank Colonel Brown. I'm only relieved that the whole affair has turned out so fortunately."

Then Cherry saw who was in the other room with Colonel Brown. It was Dr. Orchard. Mrs. Demarest murmured to Cherry that the colonel had telephoned him to come over here, for questioning. They came out of the music room together, the young doctor looking haggard and sullen—but confident!

He bowed sarcastically to Cherry. "Well! This is a pleasure, Miss Ames."

Cherry looked back at him levelly. "Dr. Orchard." She supposed he hated her now. For it was she who had uncovered his dishonesty, wrecked his ambitious plan, cost him a wealthy client.

"I can guess what you're thinking," Dr. Orchard said sullenly to Cherry, before all the others. "In a way, I admire you. You were as clever as I am myself."

Colonel Brown observed sarcastically, "You can hardly compare Lieutenant Ames with yourself, Doctor."

"I'm sorry you think I did anything wrong, madam. I cannot see that saving a dying child is wrong." But his sullen face and voice revealed his fury at being caught.

Colonel Brown studied him with shrewd eyes that had seen generations of medical people. "Saving the child of course is commendable, but weren't you—ah—also, or *primarily*, aiming at making a spectacular reputation for yourself? Dying child—prominent family—big specialists give up the case. But youthful local doctor finds the cure." She snorted and tossed her white head. "I've known unscrupulous men before."

Dr. Orchard smiled a cocky smile. "Madam, I *have* made a reputation for myself, despite everything you say. And because of the extenuating circumstances, I probably will be allowed to go on practicing. You agree, don't you? Yes. And I will also," he boasted, "get credit for developing a little known medicine."

"I think not!" Colonel Brown said sharply. "In the interests of my military patients, and of decency in the medical profession, I shall take steps to see that you get credit only for thieving. I can handle you, my smart-alecky lad!"

Cherry found herself thinking that there was something to be said in favor of battle-axes, after all!

Mrs. Demarest said, with pity in her voice, "What are you going to do now, Dr. Orchard?"

"I am planning to go to the Coast immediately after my acquittal. I have a fine offer there."

No one was cruel enough to say what they were all thinking: that he probably had no offer—that this was the traditional "staying away until the trouble blows over," unless he were sent to jail first.

Cherry wondered how Margaret Heller would feel, when she learned that her admired Dr. Orchard would allow her to face the disgrace alone. Pretty callous of him! Cherry very nearly pitied Heller, then. Cherry wondered, too, what doctor the Demarests would get for Toby now.

Colonel Brown cleared her throat, and they all jumped. "I'm leaving. You may ride back to the hospital with me, Lieutenant Ames, if you like."

THE HAPPIEST DAY

Cherry did not "like" but she obediently bade goodbye to the Demarests, nodded to Dr. Orchard, and climbed into the staff car after the doughty colonel.

A happy day had come for Jim, too. He was about to be medically discharged from the Army hospital. It hardly seemed possible to Cherry that this young man whom she had nursed and encouraged through so many stages now was to disappear out of her life. Of course she was delighted for Jim's sake that he was well and strong again—that he was about to take the final hurdle back into civilian life. There remained one more phase of rehabilitation, by which the Army could help Jim Travers.

Bright and early one morning, Cherry asked Jim to dress up and come with her.

"I'm taking you to a new start in life." She said it lightly but it was true.

"I can hardly believe I'm getting out," Jim confided, as they walked along the hospital paths under branching trees. "I'm plenty anxious, too, about how I'm going to fit in at home."

"That's what these Vocational Rehabilitation people are here for."

Cherry led Jim into the hospital's Vocation Rehabilitation office and introduced him to a man in khaki, one of many Army men behind desks. This was going to be a crucially important interview for Jim. Cherry thought she had better not intrude.

"No, don't go away, Miss Cherry," Jim said.

So Cherry sat down beside the desk and listened.

"In the first place," said the vocational guidance man, "you don't have to do anything I suggest, Sergeant Travers. You don't even have to submit to this interview, unless you want to. But maybe I can be of help to you."

Jim nodded. The vocational guidance man explained that it was his business to know what jobs were currently open all over the country. It was also his business to test Jim for the jobs he could do, or could learn to do, with the bad leg. If Jim wanted to, he could have, free of charge, a government course of training which would increase his skills and his earnings, for all the rest of his life.

"I'd like more education," Jim said eagerly.

"All right," the interviewer said. "The government will send you veterans through college, supplying you with a modest living allowance, if you'd like that, Sergeant."

Jim thought. "I'd certainly like that. But I can't afford to put off earning a good living. Guess the kind of education I want is vocational."

"All right to that too," the interviewer said. They talked it over for a while. The vocational guidance man cited cases: the musician whose badly burned hands cut him off from his profession but whom the government was training to be a teacher of music; the former truck driver who had always wanted to be a draftsman and was learning this new trade with the Army's aid; the blinded boy who was learning to become an inspector of machine parts by touch. "But of course you, Sergeant Travers, don't *have* to learn a new trade."

"I'd like to go back to woodworking," Jim said. "I like wood and I want to go back to my Oregon forests."

So, with Cherry's encouragement, he signed up for a brief, advanced course in woodworking. This he would take at the Rehabilitation Center in another state. There, too, further exercise, good food, and outdoor living would build him up to solid health. From the Rehabilitation Center, Jim would go home.

"I'm really leaving Graham," he whispered to Cherry, as the interviewer wrote out the necessary papers.

"Remember the day you arrived?" she whispered back.

"Gosh, yes! What a contrast!"

The vocational guidance man said, "Now let's go back to what we were saying at the beginning. What jobs are open—what jobs you, Jim Travers, can and want to do—and now, the third step. Now we fit you in the *right* job for you. The job where you'll do best and stay put. No hit or miss if we can help it!"

Jim said his old job was being held open for him, for a start. The interviewer dug up two other woodworking jobs in Oregon, which Jim might apply for. They could not decide. Finally Cherry suggested:

"Why don't you take time to think it over? Finish your course at the Rehabilitation Center first, and then talk it over again at a vocational office wherever you are."

"I'll write you and let you know what I decide."

"And write me how you make out on your first job." She smiled.

Jim packed that afternoon. Cherry felt badly to face this good-bye, putting it off as long as possible. She had already made train arrangements for him through the main office. Now she tucked some lunch in his pocket, had a corpsman check his heavy duffel bag through, and waited, smiling, while Jim said all the good-byes to the other men on the ward.

"All ready," he said reluctantly.

They went downstairs and started walking across the hospital grounds. Jim looked fine, erect and well in freshly pressed khaki, walking without even a cane. Cherry told him so, complimenting him.

"So you're going to be independent and take care of your mother, after all!" Cherry rejoiced. "You're valuable manpower, Jim." Even after Jim was retrained and employed, the vocational man had said, the government would give Jim further advice or training or hospital care, if he ever needed it.

Jim smiled and his face was full of sweetness. "I don't know how to thank you. Yes, I do, a little bit. Come over to the crafts shop with me, please? We have time."

There Jim piled into her arms three finely made boxes, cherry wood and rosewood and cedar, for the three members of the Ames family whom he knew. Each box was different, each beautiful.

"I wish I had a gift to give you, Jim."

"You've already given me the best gift there is. You've been my nurse."

That was something she would always remember.

They reached the Evacuation Building and went in. Then they stood in the barnlike room, Cherry with Jim's gifts in her arms, watching the wall clock tick away the last few minutes.

"You watch that leg, Jim. Keep it clean, and always wear clean stump socks. And if the artificial leg no longer fits, ask the Army for a new one."

"Yes, ma'am. You—you take care of yourself, too."

"I will. Would you—give my regards to your mother, even if I don't know her?"

Jim smiled and patted her awkwardly on the shoulder. "Yes, I will. There's my bus pulling up now."

They stood and smiled at each other, then slowly moved to the open door. They shook hands just before Jim boarded the bus.

"We won't say good-bye, Miss Cherry. Just so long."

"Just so long. Take care of yourself, Jim!"

"I'll write you. And—thanks. Thanks with all my heart."

The bus rolled off. Cherry shifted the boxes to one arm and waved frantically.

"Good luck! So long!" Her voice broke.

Jim waved from a window until the bus swerved and was hidden behind trees.

Cherry stood in the empty road, crying. She had never cried before over any patient. But never before had she experienced so profoundly the relationship of nurse and patient. Besides, these were tears of joy. She had nursed a broken, hopeless young man back to manhood.

"What a reward!" she thought. "What a reward for my work!"

She lifted her wet face proudly, and started back to her ward.

CHAPTER XV

End and Beginning

SUDDENLY IT WAS ALL OVER. CHERRY FOUND IN HER mail box at Nurses' Quarters a notice that her term of enlistment in the Army Nurse Corps—"for the duration plus six months"—was at an end. She was out of the Army! Cherry had not realized it was coming so soon—had not kept track of the dates. But here it was—and here she was—not knowing whether to be glad or sorry. She was so stunned she did not know what to think.

She ran to find Sal, who was on a ward adjoining her own.

"Sal! I've got my discharge! I'm supposed to be leaving!"

"Oh, no, Cherry," Sal said sadly. "When?"

"Right away. In a day or two, I guess."

"So soon? Do you want to leave?"

"I don't know, I don't know anything! Gosh, Sal, and I just was made chief nurse."

Sal put her arm around Cherry. "You could always re-enlist."

"Maybe I will. Maybe I ought to." Cherry shook her dark curls in bewilderment.

"I'm going soon too, I guess," Sal said. "Funny how it hurts. Never mind, I bet you'll be chief nurse some place else, I bet. And, anyhow, aren't you sort of eager to get out and try something new?"

"I don't know how I feel—it's all happening so fast. Maybe I want to stay in—My discharge, already! All I know is, I have my men to take care of—lots of them are ready to transfer to Rehabilitation Centers. Oh, Sal!" she wailed. "I'm all topsy-turvy!"

Cherry sped off to Orthopedic Ward. She told everyone her news. Patients, nurses, ward helpers crowded around her. "Aw, when?" "Shucks, no!" "Miss Cherry, we'll miss you!" "Don't go! Re-enlist—we need you!"

Cherry smiled shakily at them all, too choked up to talk. All their faces looked very dear to her. Even the brand-new wounded men—why, even the familiar white iron beds—it would be a wrench to leave them all.

Cherry glanced around at the men, counting. The Orphan, Ralph, a new patient, like herself, were soon to leave. Jim was gone. Hy Leader would have to stay on for a while. Poor Matty might be here six months or a year, though his motto was "I'll get there yet!" And here were brand-new wounded, new arrivals, lying in the beds.

"Oh, what am I to do?" Cherry thought desperately.

She went through her duties as if in a dream. Yet all she did for these men had a special urgency now—this might be the last nursing she did for these American soldiers.

How could she go off and leave them—Matty who terrified Cherry's two assistant nurses—the new patient who had come down from Operating only yesterday—the amputees, the broken, the mending ones? How could she desert them? She knew so thoroughly, now, how to run this ward, getting a top yield of efficiency out of everyone's work. Now, after months of slowly learned experience, she finally knew the best ways to talk to a wounded man, the surest methods of helping him get well. This was no time to leave, when she was more valuable to this Army hospital than ever before!

And if she left, could she be at peace with herself? Would she not be wondering how soon Hy Leader would walk again, and if Matty still had to wear his cast, and if George Blumenthal was going to teach again or not?

"These people are dear to me," Cherry thought. "They're mine—my charges. I ought to stay with them. I *want* to stay and care for them!"

And yet, as she worked daily on her ward, one incontrovertible fact stood out for Cherry. The Army Nurse Corps had said to her in effect, "You have done your full duty. You may go now, because your work here is done."

Searchingly Cherry thought back over all her Army nursing days—in many lands, in many and thrilling types of nursing. She had worked hard and faithfully, earned a decoration, kept a consistently high record.

"Yes, I suppose I have been a good soldier. But," Cherry wrestled with her conscience, "is my duty a matter of dates when my enlistment expires—or a matter of these pitiful men here still needing me?"

Doubts filled her and fought in her. Other days she saw the other side of the picture. There was other nursing to be done, outside of the Army—other people needed her, too. She tried to imagine them: men and women and children, and places, and undreamed-of situations, which the future inevitably held in store for her. Her future was moving closer and closer to her right now. The very fact that the Army Nurse Corps told her she was free to go proved that an era was over, that times were changing, from war times back into the ways of peace. Perhaps she should recognize and accept the changed tempo, move along with the times. Perhaps it was a mistake to cling to a part of her work that was done now.

"But the war is not over for these ex-soldiers lying here in these beds!" her heart cried out.

Her mind answered, "Some of these poor fellows will be chained to their beds and wheel chairs for one, two, three years more. Twenty and thirty years from now, some few of them will still be in this hospital. What are you to do, Cherry Ames? Are you to spend the rest of your life here?"

No, no, that was not the solution, either.

In desperation she fled to Sal. Evening after evening, in Cherry's room, the two girls debated all angles of the question. But when Cherry asked Sal to help her decide, Sal always said the same thing:

"No one can decide for you, Cherry. No one can ever rightly decide for another. No, you'll have to battle it through by yourself."

One day a letter from Jim arrived. It bore an Oregon postmark. Cherry was thrilled. She saved it to read on her lunch hour, and slipped back to her room to read it quietly.

It was a long letter, and a happy letter. Jim wrote movingly of his reunion with his mother, and of his profound relief to be in his own town and his own house once more. "Everything is the same," he wrote, "only now, after what I have seen and lived through in war, I value it as I never did before. Nothing has changed—only I have changed. I think I have matured."

Cherry smiled gravely at that. She too had seen war. She too had learned the full value of home and of this free, beautiful, friendly country. Perhaps—her thoughts swerved away from the letter in her hand—perhaps now that war was over, she should turn her attention and her energies to working here at home in civilian life. Even one single nurse could do a great deal toward keeping the nation healthy. If war had taught her anything, she reflected, it was to value and preserve and strengthen the ways of peace. To keep the peace! Surely building sound, healthy citizens was one of the foundations on which to build a sound, peace-preserving nation, wasn't it? But why was Jim's letter sending her off in this direction? She turned back to the closely written pages.

"—and the course in the Rehabilitation Center was wonderful. As a result of the course and the vocational placement service, I have a much better job now than I ever had before—leg or no leg! I know you'll understand my pride when I tell you I am pumping a treadle machine. The one thing I doubted I could do—and I can do it!"

Cherry did understand, and was elated about it. She thought of Jim in his tall Oregon forests, lovingly handling the raw, fragrant wood, the sound of northern rivers forever in his ears. From a burning tank to those forests, from a moaning boy on a litter to a useful, happy man, from war to peace, was a long journey, in time, space, energy, and spirit. But Jim had accomplished it—and it struck Cherry that she had better accomplish it too. She had no right to be lingering on here in the Army, against the pull of changing times. Jim's letter was making these things clear to her, very nearly making her decision for her.

"And now enough about myself," Jim wrote. "My mother wants to add something."

The handwriting changed to a round, clear, flourishing penmanship, such as Cherry had often beheld on the blackboard in her school days.

"Dear Miss Ames," Jim's mother wrote, "Jim has told me all about you. I have no way to thank you for what you did for my son. God bless you, and I hope you too will soon be back with your family. Mary A. Travers."

Cherry pressed the letter to her cheek. Those few, simple words were so honestly felt that she could almost imagine Jim's mother standing here beside her, saying, "Thank you, Cherry, for what you did for my son."

She rose now and instead of going directly to her ward, Cherry went to the hospital's main office. She told the nurse-captain there:

"Please notify Colonel Brown that Lieutenant Ames accepts her discharge from the Army Nurse Corps."

There! It was done! A load lifted from her heart, and her eyes turned to the future.

But there were still her patients to take care of, and so much to be settled for them before she went away! Ralph and the Orphan and possibly George to be got ready for transfer to the Rehabilitation Center—Matty to have the old cast taken off and a new one put on; that would take an entire afternoon's work—she would like to see a new cast on Hy Leader's leg, too, before she left—changed diets to be arranged for the new fellows, final instructions for the nurses and all the helpers on her ward—there was so much to do!

In spite of her hurry, Cherry went one last time to the Demarests'. As she entered the beautiful house, all the earlier anxiety and heartbreak and relief she had felt here for Toby came sweeping over her again. But, thank heavens, she was saying good-bye today to a child who would live!

Toby was sitting up in a chair, to Cherry's great delight. He refused to believe she was leaving.

"No more stories?" he asked, round-eyed. "No more Cherry?"

"Of course there'll be more Cherry," his young mother laughed. "After all, Cherry, you live only thirty miles away."

"If you don't come of your own accord," Mr. Demarest said, "we'll send our car over to get you. We want you to visit here, often—all of us."

"Yes!" said Toby with great emphasis. "An' I'll tell *you* a story."

"About a little boy who is getting well?" Cherry said. She kissed him, and reminisced awhile with his parents. Downstairs the rooms were full of convalescing soldiers, as usual. It was not hard to leave when she knew this was again a happy house.

The good-byes to her patients were more difficult.

Matty said, "You pestered me an awful lot but I forgive you." He blurted out, "Thanks for everything."

Cherry tugged his red hair. "Glad to get rid of you, you old toughie. Get well soon, do you hear?"

George Blumenthal shook hands with her, right-handed and proudly. "If there's ever any way my wife or I can repay you, please, please, let us know. Here, I'll write down our address for you."

He wrote it with his artificial hand, and gave it to her smiling.

Hy Leader had a quip and the Orphan a hearty handshake for her. Ralph gave her three slender silver bracelets he had made and said, "You come up to Chicago, the Pernatellis will treat you like a queen. I mean that."

Cherry laughed and joked with all of them, and suddenly fled when she felt her eyes brimming over. What good people they all were!

Sal refused to let her say good-bye. "I'll be seeing you. Say, you need a haircut." She blinked hard. "About half an inch off."

"All right, Sal," Cherry laughed. "A haircut and no good-byes."

Back and forth across the velvety green lawns, Cherry went that last afternoon. She was winding up her work but mostly she was saying good-bye to the sunny livable buildings, to the covered walks, to the squirrels, to all the GIs walking slowly in maroon bathrobes and medals.

"Good-bye, good-bye!" her heart cried out. "I still feel guilty at leaving you behind. Get well and strong and follow me soon, back to civilian life!"

"Here we rebuild men," Colonel Brown had told her when she had first arrived. Yes, Cherry had seen with her own eyes men salvaged and renewed, physically, socially, spiritually—perhaps grown stronger and more mature than ever before in their lives. What grit they had! What solid, sturdy, healthy stuff American boys were made of! To have had her own small part in helping Jim and Ralph and George and the others—this was deep satisfaction to Cherry. Well, it was done now. It was time for her to leave this place of determination, brave work, and warranted hope. The goals had been won.

Cherry took the same bus in which Jim had left. Like him, she saw one hospital building after another disappear behind trees, lost to her view.

She arrived home in Hilton at twilight, arms laden with Jim's gifts and a red-and-white cake from all the boys, flowers from Sal and a copy of *The Goldbrick* with a farewell article about Lieutenant Cherry. This was the happy-sad ending of her Army days! Her parents were waiting for her on the porch, and Midge, and Dr. Joe.

"Welcome home!" they called to her, and ran down the walk to meet her. "So you've come to an ending, Cherry."

"An end is also a beginning," she said gravely. "I'm going on from here. To what, I don't know yet—but I'm going on."